THE GIRL FROM NOWHERE

MICHELE DOMINGUEZ GREENE

Storm

Ebook ISBN: 978-1-80508-815-8
Paperback ISBN: 978-1-80508-817-2

Cover design: Blacksheep
Cover images: Depositphotos, Shutterstock

Published by Storm Publishing.
For further information, visit:
www.stormpublishing.co

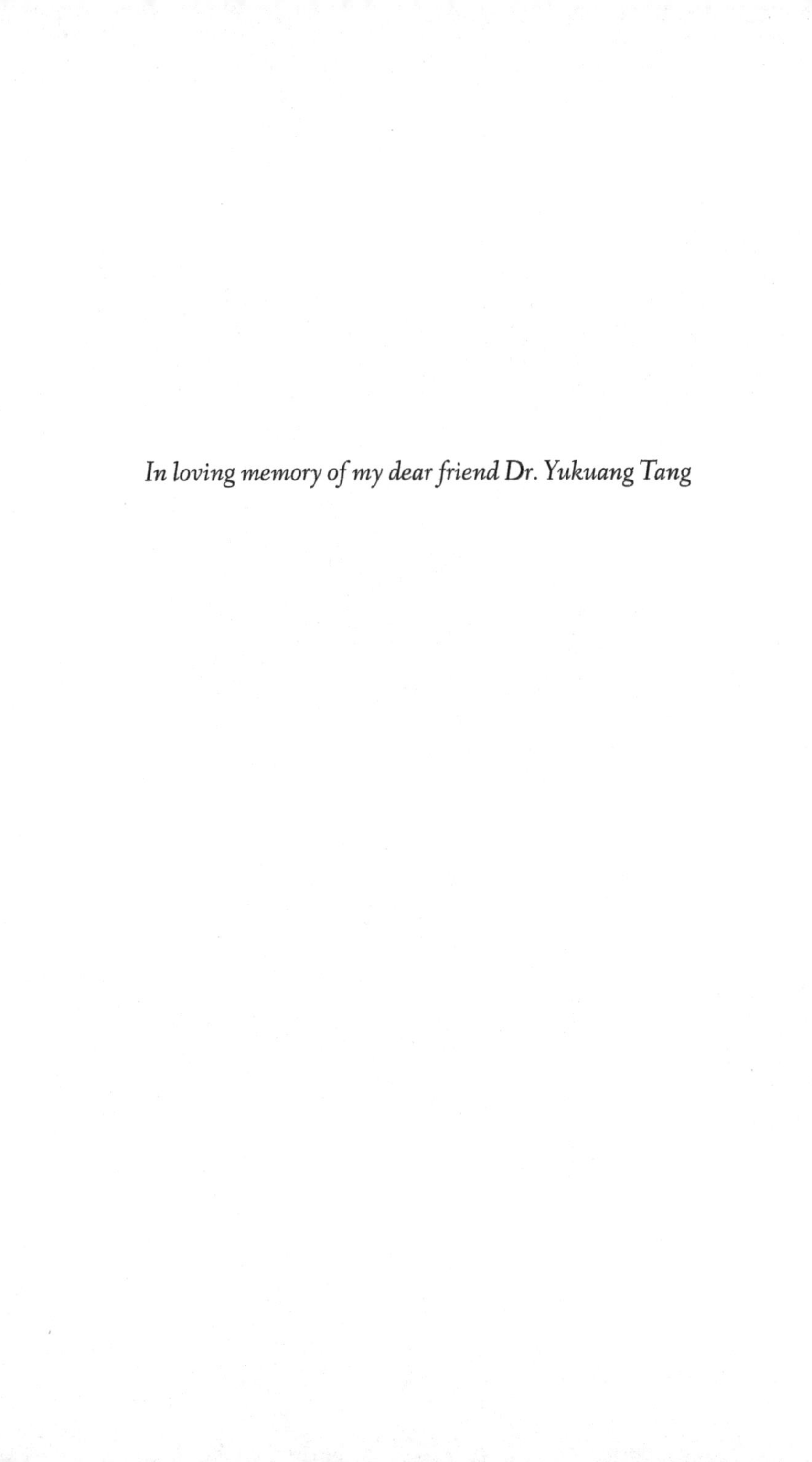

In loving memory of my dear friend Dr. Yukuang Tang

PROLOGUE

The toddler wouldn't stop crying. She was pitching a fit, kicking and screaming, on the flagstone pool deck. The tall cypress trees stood guard around the sparkling blue infinity pool; a thick hedge of hibiscus filled the air with a sweet, heady aroma. The girl in the green bathing suit didn't even remember what triggered the meltdown. She lay on the chaise, a magazine over her eyes, shielding her from the bright midday sun. The child was still crying, jagged, heaving sobs and shrieks. Why didn't someone come from the big house to help with her? They had to hear her. They should come and take the kid inside, where the girl wouldn't have to listen to her. Just for a little while. The girl's head was pounding, her eyelids felt scratchy, as if she had sand under them. Even with her eyes shut and covered, the sun was burning them. She hated that feeling.

She needed another hit; she felt her nerves getting ragged. She preferred hot railing but that took too much effort, and she'd been feeling dope sick all day. She reached under the chaise and pulled out her little satchel that held her bowl pipe and crystal meth. She sat up, took a hit and stashed the satchel under the chaise cushion. She inhaled deeply and lay back down, the drug flooding her brain with such sweet release.

But the child hadn't stopped carrying on. The little girl waddled over to the chaise, her chubby legs unsteady and her sticky hands grasping at the girl's legs, reaching for her. The girl pushed her away, not today. But the child wouldn't stop, she grabbed at the girl's golden hair and tugged on it, hard. She pushed the child away again. The sound of her small footsteps padding away on the pavement, searching for some other fun. Then it was quiet. So blissfully quiet. The girl breathed easily, the methamphetamine enveloping her in a dopamine cloud. The beautiful silence felt like heaven. The sun was warm on her skin. She felt as if she were floating.

A pair of hands on her shoulders, shaking her violently. A woman's face she recognized but couldn't place was close to hers, shouting.

"What happened? Weren't you watching?"

The girl shook her head, trying to understand what the woman was saying. She was wet, dripping water from her hair and clothing; at her feet lay the child. The little girl looked like a doll but her skin was so white, like flour.

"What did you do? Tell me!" The woman shook her harder.

"Stop! I didn't do anything..." the girl protested. But had she? She couldn't remember.

The woman sobbed, scooping up the child and clutching her tightly, carrying her toward the house.

Running now, the woman was screaming for help. The girl heard her voice as if it were coming from the far end of a long tunnel. Rising and falling like a dime store slide whistle.

"Get help! She's still breathing!"

The woman ran, cresting the grassy hill that led to the big house. The child was breathing... but the girl watched as her arm hung limply, a thin branch of white birch. She knew somehow that she should follow them and stood on her unsteady legs. She began walking up the hill, but lost her balance and fell, biting her tongue, tasting blood in her mouth. She tried to stand but couldn't. She crawled but her strength gave out and she lay back. She felt like she was spinning, on the grass, staring at the sun above her like a golden mandala...

ONE

Emily Ray sat at the counter in her big kitchen, the sunlight streaming through the windows that looked out to the expansive garden, still glistening with dew from the morning marine layer that hung over the city. She was strategically building a pile of almond biscotti into a structure with her two seven-year-old daughters, Juliana and Eliza.

"When it gets tall enough, we'll put a napkin on as the roof!" Juli said excitedly as Liza began folding one into the right shape. Moose, their Mastiff mix, sat below the counter, hoping for a tidbit of a cookie to fall in his direction.

Emily checked the TV schedule again; she had to watch a segment of the morning news show, *The World Today*, with anchorwoman Jasmin Lourdes, at the request of her boss at the FBI, SAC John Powers. He was putting her on a case that related to the unexpected return of the young heiress to the Doucette-Browne fortune, Kaveri Miller Browne. Kaveri had been kidnapped as a child but was now back, eighteen years later. Powers had asked Emily to investigate the legitimacy of her identity. But he had given her scant details and instructed her to watch an interview with Kaveri and her grandmother, Mackenzie Miller

Browne, the matriarch of the prominent family. He would brief her on the investigation when she arrived at the office.

She was up early, to drive the twins to school on her way to work. She knew her husband, Antonio, would be up shortly but she made sure to carve out some extra time with her daughters.

"Mommy, can you get a gingerbread house kit at Trader Joe's? I saw them last week when we went with Dolores. I think a real kit would make a better house for Santa," Liza suggested.

"This is just a trial run, it's not really a house." Emily laughed as Antonio entered, dressed for work in his usual khakis and polo shirt. His black hair was still damp from the shower.

"What's going on? An architectural extravaganza?" he asked, picking up a biscotti.

"We're making an office building, like JPL," Juli said, referring to Antonio's place of work, Jet Propulsion Lab.

"That's kind of complicated, isn't it?" he said, turning to Emily. "How'd you sleep?"

"Fine, you?" she replied.

"You bet Mommy slept good without you snoring in her ear all night, Daddy!" Liza laughed.

Emily and Antonio exchanged a brief look; since they'd decided to separate, they'd continued sharing the family home to avoid disrupting Juli and Liza's lives. Using the pretext of his snoring, Antonio had quietly moved into one of the guest bedrooms.

"Yes, I'm sure she slept much better," Antonio said, settling onto the kitchen stool next to Emily and leaning in for a morning kiss, which she deflected as she did every day by standing up and moving to the sink with the breakfast dishes. It was like a new dance they had developed, two people swirling around each other in a domestic space but never really connecting. Emily saw a fleeting shadow of disappointment on her husband's face, but she wasn't ready to move forward and make everything right between them. She wasn't sure she would ever be, after his infidelity, six months earlier.

"We could try to bake our own gingerbread and cut it into

pieces to make a house," Antonio's aunt, Dolores, suggested, adding Famous Amos cookies to the girls' lunch packs.

"No way! We tried that last year," Liza moaned, carefully setting a biscotti on the roof of the structure.

"That is too much for our skill set," Juli said. "Ms. Goodwin said we have to work within our skill set." The biscotti building tumbled down in ruins onto the counter.

"No!" shouted Juli.

"At least each one is wrapped in plastic so there are no crumbs to clean up," added Liza, ever the practical planner.

"What time will you be back from work?" Antonio asked Emily as he poured his coffee.

"Not late. I'm getting a new case today, Powers emailed me late last night," Emily replied.

Antonio nodded. "Another kidnapping?"

Emily knew he was digging for information that she no longer shared with him. Her return to the FBI had been unstructured; she hadn't decided on a new division after her decision to leave CARD after many years as the head of that team. But since the separation, she didn't discuss such things with Antonio.

"No. I don't have all the details. He asked me to watch *The World Today* this morning. The case has to do with an heiress who reappeared after being kidnapped years ago," Emily said, evenly, making it clear that there would be no further discussion. It was as if certain parts of her life were now off limits to him. He nodded, keenly aware of the boundary she set. Dolores cast a troubled glance at them and the girls.

"I'll be getting the Christmas decorations from the garage today," Dolores said, with forced cheerfulness. "I'm thinking we can decorate the house and put up the tree this week."

"Yes!" the girls shouted, jumping up and down.

"Is it that time already?" Antonio asked. "It's been almost six months."

Emily shot him a warning look; they had agreed not to talk

about the state of their marriage in front of Juli and Liza. Not until something had been decided.

"Six months since what?" Emily asked. "Since summer?"

He nodded. "Yeah. Since summer. Seems like yesterday we were making vacation plans."

"They've got the trees for sale in the lots over by the freeway. I saw them a few days ago. They have a lot of different types of trees," Dolores interrupted.

"That'll be fun. We'll pick one up," Emily agreed, avoiding Antonio's gaze. She changed the television station to CBS for *The World Today*, and set it to record mode, as she ushered the girls out of the kitchen.

"Go brush your teeth and get your backpacks ready. Mommy has to watch a show for work and then we're leaving," she said, refilling her coffee mug from the French press on the counter. Antonio slid his cup across to her, but she let him fill it on his own, one of the small considerations lost between them. Dolores sensed the tension between Emily and Antonio and kept busy, putting utensils away. She'd lived with them since the twins were born and this was the first time there had been a rift in their marriage. Everyone was adjusting to the new normal.

"Since it's almost Christmas, maybe we should figure out how to move forward, Emily—"

She cut him off mid-sentence, "Now is not the time to talk about all of that; we're getting ready to go to school. We'll discuss it in private. I have to watch this segment on *The World Today*. Kaveri Miller Browne returned home alive and my new case has something to do with it," she said, settling in with her notebook and pen ready.

They watched the opening credits of the show with glamorous news anchor Jasmin Lourdes seated on a cozy couch, next to a heavyset man and Kaveri and Mackenzie Miller Browne.

Jasmin Lourdes looked deep into the camera, her dark eyes dripping with empathy and gravitas.

"Eighteen years ago, two-year-old Kaveri Miller Browne, an heir to the vast fortune of the Doucette-Browne family was abducted from their estate in Holmby Hills. The search for her spanned years and involved the LAPD, the FBI and private investigators. Despite an exhaustive search, they came up empty-handed and the family was left to deal with the devastating loss. Until retired LAPD detective, Rawley Jaynes, finally tracked Kaveri down, never giving up on what many considered, a hopeless case," Lourdes said in her carefully calibrated news anchor voice.

"This hits kind of close to home, doesn't it?" Antonio asked.

"I think that's why Powers wants me on it," Emily replied, not taking her eyes from the television.

While Jasmin Lourdes filled in the background of the case, Emily watched Kaveri and Mackenzie Browne. They sat side by side, Mackenzie holding Kaveri's hand in support. Mackenzie appeared calm and unflappable, accustomed to a life of presenting the proper image to the public. Kaveri, in contrast, was clearly nervous, tapping her foot, blinking repeatedly in the glare of the bright lights of the studio. Mackenzie wore an unstructured dark suit and a silk blouse, Kaveri a fitted but modestly cut knee-length dress in deep purple. They both presented an image of coordinated elegance and restrained style, signatures of the Doucette-Browne identity.

"Can you describe the emotions you felt when Mr. Jaynes called to say he had found your granddaughter?" Lourdes asked Mackenzie.

Mackenzie looked down at her hands, composing herself and biting back emotion, she said, "It felt like I'd been struck by lightning, really. After all these years. I knew Rawley was still searching but you just... give up any hope, you know? And even when I spoke to her on a FaceTime call, I was afraid to believe it. Do you remember that, Kaveri?"

Kaveri nodded, nervously, and said, "It was kind of weird. I mean, I'd been living this totally different life. I thought a different woman was my mom, I had no idea. I didn't even know who the Doucette-Browne family was. Mr. Jaynes told me and he took a DNA swab from me, to be sure."

"And it came back as a match?" Lourdes said, dropping her voice dramatically.

"Yes, it was a match," Mackenzie said, as tears began to spill down her cheeks.

Lourdes handed her a tissue and continued. "I can't imagine. But, Mr. Jaynes, you've really made a mission of these cases. After retiring from the LAPD, you've devoted yourself to finding these victims, right?"

Rawley Jaynes nodded. He was built like a cinderblock; his thick neck was so short, it looked as if his head was sitting on his shoulders, like a pig on a platter in a medieval feast.

"It's hard to sleep at night, knowing that some of these people went missing as children and have never been found. Once a case goes cold, it's over, no matter what law enforcement says. So, I just put my nose to the grindstone and start digging."

"You have a new book to promote called *Home at Last*, covering your work on the Kaveri Miller Browne case, but you also have another success story for us, correct?"

"Yes, I've located another woman who went missing as a child and was never found. She's here tonight to share her story," Jaynes said with a self-satisfied grin.

"I know we are all anxious to hear from her," Lourdes said, standing to welcome the new guest. A blond woman in her late thirties walked onstage. Unlike Mackenzie and Kaveri, this woman wore clothes that were generic and slightly out of date. Emily knew she must have worn her best outfit for the appearance and felt a pang of sympathy for the woman as she smiled awkwardly at the audience. Her blond hair was pulled back in a simple ponytail and she twisted her hands nervously in her lap as she took her seat next to Mackenzie and Kaveri. Lourdes smiled broadly as she shook her hand and turned to the studio audience with a flourish.

"Please welcome Danica Hansen!"

Emily dropped the coffee cup she was holding, paying no attention as it shattered on the floor, the dark liquid spreading across the tile like a bloodstain.

TWO

Emily sat frozen, staring at the screen, as Dolores approached with a dishrag to clean up the coffee that was pooling beneath the counter. She'd heard the cup fall and break; she tapped Emily's shoulder, concerned.

"Emilia, *mija...* are you alright?" she asked, looking nervously at her nephew who sat across from his wife, his eyes glued to Emily's reaction.

Emily turned to Dolores with a start. "Uh... I'm fine, Dolores. I was... just shocked for a moment... here, I can do that," she said, taking the dishrag from her and kneeling down to clean up. She welcomed the moment to look away from the people on the television screen and the concerned attention of her family. She wiped the coffee up and walked to the sink, like a zombie, wringing the dishrag out under the cold running water, listening to the voices on the news show, saying things she could not believe or comprehend. She returned to the kitchen counter to watch in horror as the show continued.

"I began looking into Danica's case, wondering how a little girl could just disappear into thin air. There were a lot of missteps by the police in the South Bay and not a lot of attention given to her case, to be honest. Just a few years before, Emily Ray was abducted from the same area, within a mile away, which generated a ton of leads and attention due to her family's wealth, but Danica's case didn't," Rawley Jaynes explained. "And of course, Emily Ray returned home eight years later, alive and well."

Emily felt her stomach clench and begin to roil at his words.

Danica Hansen... Emily Ray... taken from the same area... returned home eight years later...

Antonio reached out for her hand and this time she didn't have the presence of mind to push him away. She sat stock-still, unmoving, watching the reaction of the woman on the screen who was pretending to be her. The woman who had falsely claimed her real identity as Danica Hansen. The whole thing was like a nightmare, the kind she had suffered her entire life. She quickly began jotting down notes, as Antonio moved to her. Dolores hovered but he signaled to her that they needed privacy and the older woman reluctantly left to check on Juli and Liza.

"Are you okay, Em?" he asked quietly.

She shook her head silently, her eyes glued to the blond woman seated beside Mackenzie and Kaveri, self-consciously gripping her hands together.

"I don't have a lot of childhood memories, to be honest. I know that I went to live with my parents, Hilda and Roy, when I was about eleven years old," Danica Hansen said. Emily felt light-headed and nauseous listening to her fabricated story.

"And prior to that?" Lourdes asked.

"I lived with Hilda's cousin, Coralee Buell. I thought she was my mom, but she always said she wasn't and wouldn't let me call her that. But I can't recall a lot of details. They are very hazy."

"You've had epilepsy since you were born, correct?" Lourdes asked.

"Yeah. I've always had to take medication, and I've lost a lot of memories, so I have to rely on what people tell me happened in the past," Danica said, self-consciously.

Emily sat up, "Epilepsy? Where'd they come up with that? This is insane!"

Antonio placed his hand on her arm to steady her; she ignored him, her attention fixed on the television.

"Yes," Danica continued, "and once I went to live with Roy and Hilda Sanders, they became my family. I still live with them."

"Even now that you know your real mother is Amber Hansen? Was that strange for you?" Lourdes asked, leaning into her.

Danica's eyes darted to Jaynes for guidance or reassurance. Emily watched closely, there was something in the woman's narrative that made her uncomfortable. She clearly didn't like the attention and scrutiny of being on a national news show. Emily made furious notes, scanning Mackenzie and Kaveri Miller Browne for any sense that they knew the woman beside them was a fraud.

Jaynes took Danica's hand. In a voice thick with emotion, he said, "People always think kids have been taken by criminals and predators. Sometimes, it's just people who see a struggling kid and want to help. Or they stay in an imperfect situation for a time and then get away, and often, they don't remember who they were originally. So, they kind of exist at the margins of society."

Emily slapped the counter, pulling herself out of a stunned state of shock.

"Jesus Christ! What is this guy saying? Kids are taken in by good Samaritans who just want to help? This is bullshit," she mumbled, jumping to her feet, pacing back and forth. Antonio touched her arm again, to stop her. She shook his hand away.

"Emily, you have to calm down. Clearly this guy is a fraud, and that woman is not Danica Hansen if you are."

"What do you mean 'if'? Of course I'm Danica Hansen. I wasn't taken at two years old. I was ten, I remember who I was before Tibbs got me."

"I just mean, that if you're investigating this Browne girl's identity and you know the detective is a fraud, there's a good chance that she is as well," he said, calmly, trying to steady her.

"He's full of shit and I don't know how he's gotten anyone to go along with all of this. I have to find out everything I can about this Rawley Jaynes guy, and this woman who's pretending to be me. I'm sure Kaveri Browne is a fake as well. But I can't march into John Powers' office and say, 'I know the whole thing is a fraud because I'm really Danica Hansen.' Can I? You were the one who said that would cause so many problems in every way and there was no real reason to come clean about it." She spoke at a rapid-fire pace, the words running over one another. Antonio waited a moment before speaking, gauging her emotional state.

"Do you think it might be time to tell Lydia the truth about who you are? So, she can help you navigate this?" he suggested gently.

Emily had only confided her true identity to him a few months earlier, in the wake of the Josie Vance kidnapping case. Her long-time therapist, Lydia Walsh, had no idea that she was not the real Emily Ray, a teenager who had died twenty-three years ago while both girls were held by child predator, James Tibbs. But she had chosen to keep her identity as Danica Hansen, abducted at ten years old, a secret from Lydia. She wasn't ready to reveal the truth yet.

Now Emily scoffed bitterly. "No way! I'm not telling her, ever. I told you and look what happened?"

"Em, I've told you repeatedly, your identity had nothing to do with what happened in Arizona, with Anjelica. That was all my bullshit, okay? You didn't cause that in any way," he said.

"Right. Prior to that, we had a perfect marriage, didn't we? Then I told you and within a few months you were hooking up with a woman you hadn't seen in years. Don't tell me it's not related. So, no, I'm not telling Lydia. I can't risk losing another person I love," she said.

"You haven't lost me. I want this to work, I want..."

She interrupted him, "Please, I'm not going there right now. I have to get to work, to find out from Powers what all of this is about. I'll watch the rest of the show on my iPad. I can't sit still here... I just can't!"

She left the room abruptly and gathered her briefcase, unlocking the gun safe to slide her Glock into her shoulder holster.

"C'mon, girls! It's time to go!" she called out as Dolores brought them into the kitchen. She looked from Antonio to Emily, uncertain and worried.

"Is everything okay?" she asked, tentatively.

Emily squeezed her hand and smiled warmly at her, "It's fine. Are we all ready to go?" She knew how to cover; compartmentalizing her emotions was a superpower she perfected in captivity with James Tibbs and living with a false identity for her entire adult life.

She followed the girls toward the front door as Dolores pushed her lunch pack into her hands.

"You're forgetting your lunch, *mija*," Dolores said.

"Thank you. I just have a lot on my mind today, starting a new case," Emily explained, not meeting her eyes.

"That's 'cause Mommy's a badass and that's not a bad word. It means donkey," Juli explained as they walked out the door to Emily's Mercedes GLC waiting in the long driveway.

Emily laughed awkwardly, wishing her daughter's words were true. At the moment, with her nerves in a raw jangle of tension, her mind racing over a million possibilities, she felt like anything but a badass and more like a basket case.

Rawley Jaynes rode in the back of the town car, sent courtesy of CBS to shuttle him to and from *The World Today* studio. Beside him sat his assistant and erstwhile girlfriend, Zanie Lichtman, her hand resting on his thigh. He smiled to himself; the interview had gone exceptionally well. Kaveri and Mackenzie were great, and Danica managed to pull herself through it without any major mistakes. Zanie was scrolling on her iPad, a smile spreading across her face.

"It's happening just like we predicted, Rawley! Tons of messages and requests coming through the website," she said excitedly.

She looked to him with admiration; they had pulled it off. The whole thing was their master plan, dreamed up after Mackenzie contacted Jaynes with yet another request for help with a family problem. Tired of being at Mackenzie's beck and call, they had come up with an idea that would springboard them into a whole new lucrative career: solving cold cases and finding long-missing individuals that everyone had given up on. His new book and the television appearance were the first steps to realizing that goal. And Jaynes had what Mackenzie needed for her to go along with the plan. He'd have to deliver it into her grasping, well-manicured hands before the end of the day, to hold up his part of the bargain.

Jaynes unbuttoned his suit jacket; it was straining over his large belly. He let out a sigh of relief as the fabric gave way and he could breathe easily. He was glad to have taken Zanie's advice and worn the steel-gray, monochrome suit combination rather than the electric-purple he would have chosen on his own. She said he had to start looking the part of a serious investigator and not like a flashy L.A. Vice cop. He ran his thick fingers through his platinum, spiked hair, making it stand up even higher. He looked to Zanie, thinking that they made a sharp-looking couple, and she never questioned any of his shadier business arrangements. She was a good partner, for now.

Zanie was petite, barely five feet tall with black curly hair that she meticulously straightened every morning. She'd had an aggressive rhinoplasty at sixteen that left her looking like the elfin sister to Snap, Crackle and Pop from the Rice Krispies cereal box. She wore perfectly coordinated outfits with matching accessories, from her diamond stud earrings to her dainty gold chain, always a signature brooch just below her clavicle. Her look was calculated to show class and restraint, elegance over opulence, which helped balance out his natural flair for all things bright and shiny. She was good at handling the details; he was a people person who knew how to work a room and sell a product, especially himself.

"So, how many inquiries are we getting? It's not even been half a day!" he remarked, with satisfaction.

"Listen to this, 'Mr. Jaynes, I just saw you on *The World Today* and I want to talk to you about finding my sister, Heather, who has been missing for the past three years. Please call me, blah, blah, blah.' And there are probably fifty just like it, we're not even back home yet!" Zanie exclaimed, impressed.

"This is a business plan that's like the old well on my grandpa's farm. A bottomless source of sustenance," he said, loosening his belt and reaching for the bag of Corn Nuts he pilfered from his dressing room hospitality basket at CBS. He popped them into his mouth with a loud crunch. "Are we hitting Denny's for breakfast?"

"You don't need a Grand Slam, honey. Not if you're going to be doing press and meeting clients. It's time to start a diet and exercise routine. This is L.A. and no one has confidence in a fat guy, okay?" she said, bluntly.

Jaynes pouted and stared out the window. She was right, as usual. He'd have to get himself into top form if he wanted to entice wealthy families to pay for his services, and even the not so wealthy ones. He didn't care if they were filthy rich like the Doucette-Brownes or teetering at the edge of working-class respectability like Danica's parents. He just wanted their money. And now it looked like he would be getting a whole lot of it, if everyone played the game.

THREE

Mackenzie Miller Browne poured herself another cup of Guatemalan Antigua Reserve from her French press. It was ninety-five dollars for a five-pound bag, but she could afford it. It felt good to have *The World Today* news segment over. They had been planning it for the past several weeks and she'd been working with Kaveri to prepare her for the media attention that would follow. It was the final step of Kaveri's introduction to the world, claiming her spot as the rightful heir to the Doucette-Browne fortune. Mackenzie savored those words as they played over and over again in her head.

The rightful heir...

Now, there would be a flurry of interest from the press and the public, paparazzi would camp outside the family compound, hoping to catch a glimpse of the young heiress, and write about her Cinderella story. With Kaveri back, everything was falling into place, exactly as it should.

At fifty-seven, Mackenzie was the youngest and only surviving child of her father, Gerald "Jinx" Doucette-Browne. The product of his third failed marriage, her half-siblings had all self-destructed. Tragedy hung over the family like a cerement of the grave. Mackenzie took a long sip of her coffee, savoring the rich, dark flavor. She looked out the big picture window to the expanse of lawn where she had occasionally played with her much older siblings. Her memories of childhood were filled with the ghosts of her tragic siblings and the treacherous terrain of the survival sport that they called family life in the Doucette-Browne compound. She could still see them, in every corner of the big house, on the perfectly manicured grounds.

Teenaged J.J. swinging a bat at a ball tossed by the family chauffeur, Morton... he missed, his gangly limbs loose and awkward... Jinx seated in the shade of the big magnolia tree, dressed in a seersucker suit...

"Can't you do anything right, for fuck's sake? It's just a ball, how hard is it to hit? My God, you're as clumsy as a buffalo!" he shouted at J.J., springing out of his Adirondack chair, running to the teenager and swatting him in the head with an open palm...

"Thank heavens I have money because you can't do anything right. You're just a nothing and to think I gave you my name..."

Twelve-year-old Jasper was locked in his room for three days with no food as punishment for some banal and childish trespass, crying and banging on the closed door as Mackenzie sat in the hallway helpless and terrified, while the staff hurried by with their eyes down...

Emmeline Amaya, standing up in front of all the guests at the big Christmas party, like her father asked her to...

"Look at that mess! What girl would choose a dress that makes her ass look like a football field!" Jinx shouted, drunk and belligerent, as Emmeline Amaya's face crumpled in shame... and later, in the big kitchen pantry, Mackenzie found her cutting the dress to shreds with poultry shears while still wearing it... each slash was like a wound being opened on her frail body...

Mackenzie shook off the memories. There were countless others. They grew up surrounded by luxury but crippled and broken emotionally by their father's abuse. The wives fared better, they were able to divorce and obtain big financial settlements, but they insisted their children stay within the Doucette-Browne fold, riding out the rough waves to inherit their piece of the obscenely large pie.

Once her siblings died, Mackenzie was the last combatant standing. She only had one child left, Sierra, who had been in and out of rehab countless times but at least she was alive. Mackenzie's favorite, Connor, had died twenty years earlier from mainlining bad heroin. Within a year, her only granddaughter, Kaveri, had been abducted. It had been a long, dry drought season in her life without any good news.

Now Jinx was bedridden and confused most days, cared for by an attendant. Mackenzie showed up twice a week for the obligatory visit to sit by his bedside, where he lay like a corpse, covered up to his neck in crisp white sheets, his liver-spotted hands clutching at the covers. He had brief moments of clarity that would evaporate like water drops on a hot skillet. She asked questions and had no interest in his answers.

How are you feeling today, Daddy?

Did you enjoy the soup that Chef Michel made?

You should get Gerte to push your wheelchair out to the gardens now that the flowers are blooming.

She smiled, remembering the day she showed him the DNA results for Kaveri, once Jaynes had located the girl. Mackenzie couldn't tell if her father was pleased or disappointed, his blue eyes as empty as marbles when she showed him the results from the DNA lab on her phone screen. It didn't matter if he understood or not. Kaveri was back. And today, Jaynes was bringing by the hard copies of those results as promised. After so many years of loss and sorrow, it was a miracle, really. She owed it all to Rawley Jaynes, who had investigated the case eighteen years earlier.

Kaveri was a stranger to all of them; she'd disappeared when she was two and had no memories of living inside the compound of the big house, which was Jinx's residence. The other stately homes on the multi-acre property were for his long-dead offspring, but now Kaveri, at twenty-years-old, would move into whichever one caught her fancy.

She heard Kaveri coming down the big staircase, her young voice so filled with energy and optimism. It sounded strangely out of place in the hushed, sterile elegance of Mackenzie's home.

"Are you heading out to do some shopping, Kaveri? I made a list of the stores and shops you should start frequenting. You won't need any money, we have accounts at all of them so you can simply charge whatever you want," Mackenzie said.

"Thank you, Grandmother. I'd like to go pick up a few new things," Kaveri said as the head housekeeper, Gerte, followed behind her. She was getting used to saying "grandmother." She'd made the mistake of referring to Mackenzie as "grandma" once and it was pointed out to her that it sounded common and low class. The proper way to say it was "grandmother."

"Gerte will go with you today, but we'll arrange for one of our security staff to accompany you on trips outside the compound from now on. You'll have to be extra careful now that people know what you look like. They'll start following you, trying to engage you in conversation or some other nonsense. None of those strangers are your friends, dear. You must remember that. They are bottom-feeders looking for some angle to extort you, blackmail you, and get money from you."

Kaveri nodded obediently, her enthusiasm withering. Mackenzie took her hand, warmly, and pushed a stray piece of hair behind Kaveri's ear.

"I'm not trying to frighten you, dear. It's just your new reality. Everyone wants something from you once they know about this family. You can't trust anyone. You'll get used to it."

Gerte led the way to the black town car that was waiting for them outside. Kaveri cast a nervous glance around the house before following Gerte and disappearing into the car, invisible through the dark, tinted windows. Mackenzie watched the car drive away with relief. She didn't want Kaveri home when Rawley Jaynes came over. In fact, from now on, she wanted Jaynes as far away from her granddaughter as possible.

FOUR

Danica Hansen drove her 2005 Hyundai on the crowded 101 Freeway, confused by the many interchanges that she needed to get her to Highway 15, toward home, in Baker California. She had only been to Los Angeles twice before and it was overstimulating to her: the traffic, the people, the noise and sense of everything swirling around her at high speed. She felt light-headed but she figured it was just the excitement and lack of sleep. She'd arrived the previous day to stay at a hotel in Studio City, courtesy of *The World Today* program. They needed her in the studio for the news segment with Mr. Jaynes early in the morning. She didn't really want to appear on television; the attention made her uncomfortable. She had never been someone in the spotlight; if anything, she preferred hiding in the shadows.

The green freeway signs showed several different connections, and she took the wrong one, heading toward The L.A. Zoo rather than San Bernardino. She pulled off at an exit that led to a Train Museum, adjacent to the freeway. Panicking at her mistake, she pulled into the parking lot of the Train Museum to get her bearings. She wished her mother, Hilda, had been able to come with her for moral support, but her dad, Roy, was feeling particularly bad that week and couldn't be left alone. Danica took a deep breath and parked her car under the shade of a big oak tree, double checking the route to the 210 Freeway that would lead her to the 15, toward home. She leaned back in her seat and closed her eyes. She could feel her heart still pounding in her chest.

The television show had been stressful; she didn't like the makeup artist touching her face or the way the costume lady's lips got tight and thin when she looked at the outfits Danica had brought with her. Everything felt like playacting.' And she struggled with that feeling all the time since Mr. Jaynes had showed up at her work, months earlier, shadowing her on the casino floor of Whiskey Pete's just over the Nevada border. She worked in the cage, counting money, and one day Mr. Jaynes was there, hanging around.

Eventually, he spoke to her about his suspicions that she might be Danica Hansen who was kidnapped years before from Redondo Beach. She didn't believe him but he kept insisting until she finally agreed to a DNA test which proved he was right.

The past few months had been a challenge, coming to terms with the fact that she was someone else and not Shirelle Sanders. The only good thing to come from being Danica Hansen was the money. Mr. Jaynes told them it came from a victim's fund that the state paid out and it had given them the means to try a new, experimental treatment for her father's cancer which had gotten worse. Roy was diagnosed with aggressive stage three non-Hodgkin lymphoma. Money was tight and they had been reeling from her dad's health insurance denying his treatment with a new, experimental drug.

Her phone rang; she saw that it was Zanie, Rawley Jaynes' girlfriend.

"Hello, Zanie, is everything okay?" Danica asked. She realized that she always asked this when Zanie or Rawley called, as if she were waiting for bad news.

"Yes, everything is fine, honey. Are you on your way home?" Zanie asked.

"Yeah. I got a little confused on the freeways, but I think I know where to go now."

"And how's your dad?"

She always asked, which Danica appreciated. "He's doing okay. He starts the new treatment in nine days."

"I'm sure that will work out well for him. I just wanted you to know that you did great on the show today. We may be setting up some more appearances to tell the story of how Rawley found you and Kaveri, and to promote his book. Maybe some television shows, some magazines with photos. It's going to be a lot of fun!" Zanie said.

Danica felt her heart drop. She didn't want to do any more shows like *The World Today* because she couldn't quite make sense of the whole story. But she felt grateful for the money from the victim's fund, so she made the best of it, especially if it helped Mr. Jaynes to promote his book.

"Sure, that sounds fun," Danica said half-heartedly, before hanging up.

She pulled her car out of the lot and onto the freeway. She found her way to the right interchange and sighed in relief when she was on the correct road that led toward home. Perhaps it wasn't so bad to be on TV or in magazines sometimes. Mr. Jaynes had helped in his way to generate the money for Roy. There were a lot of questions she didn't have answers to, things that didn't really add up in the back of her mind. But if it might save her dad's life, it didn't matter at all.

Emily sat in traffic on the 405 Freeway, on the last leg of her commute to the FBI offices in Westwood. She had stopped at a Starbucks for a venti Americano and watched the remainder of *The World Today* segment on her iPad in the parking lot. She stared at Kaveri Miller Browne, the missing child miraculously returned, just as she had been twenty-three years earlier. But Kaveri Miller Browne didn't have the same secret hanging over her like the blade of a guillotine. She was out in the public eye, front and center, claiming her place in the Doucette-Browne rarified universe.

SAC Powers had given Emily just the barest information regarding the investigation, but she knew it hinged on the veracity of Kaveri Browne's identity. Just the thought of it made Emily queasy, digging into the background of a young woman who'd been missing for years. If anyone had done the same for her, when she returned as Emily Ray after escaping James Tibbs, they might have discovered the truth.

The fear of being discovered had haunted her her entire life and it still shadowed her, even when there was no way anyone could ever find out now, with Tibbs dead. Only she and Antonio knew the truth and even though their marriage was falling apart, she knew he would never reveal her secret about who she really was. But now she felt a sense of outrage that someone else was claiming that identity falsely.

She knew her feelings made no sense. She knew that surviving the kind of trauma she'd faced as a child meant she would find herself caught in illogical spirals of emotion and fear. But she was shaken. It was like a whisper from beyond the grave. *Danica Hansen.*

Emily feared the girl she had once been would never let her go.

FIVE

Special Agent in Charge, John Powers, sat at his desk in the FBI offices in the Federal Building. His assistant buzzed to let him know Special Agent Emily Ray had arrived for her briefing. He'd called her the previous evening to alert her that he had a new case for her, after receiving a phone call he wished he had missed. It had come in late from his old friend and college buddy, Senator Harry Hubbard, of North Carolina.

"*I've got a favor to ask, John. You know my longtime friend, Jinx Doucette-Browne?*" Hubbard asked with his usual Southern ease.

"*I don't know him personally, but I certainly know of him.*"

"*And you remember the kidnapping of Jinx's granddaughter, Kaveri?*"

"*Yes. I wasn't at the bureau yet, but it was very high profile.*"

"*It was a tragedy, just unthinkable.*"

"*But she was never found,*" Powers said.

"*That's just it. It's about to break all over the news that Kaveri Miller Browne has been found, after eighteen years missing, and I'd like you to make sure she's legit, you know? To protect my old pal, Jinx, from any shenanigans. There are so many crooks.*"

"*Wouldn't this be something for you to run by the office in D.C.? Since you're a sitting senator?*" Powers asked.

"Nah, nah, this is a personal request, John. You understand?"

Powers understood perfectly. Hubbard didn't want the Washington office of the FBI involved because it would be too easy to trace. He had to go through back channels for this type of thing.

"Sure, that's no problem, Harry. We'll look into this and make sure everything is as it should be for Mr. Doucette-Browne," Powers assured him.

"Terrific and we'll just keep this between us, alright? You can call me directly to let me know what you've found out. And when you're ready to retire, we'll have to talk. I know some big players who'd love to have you on their executive board!" Hubbard said, with a hearty, hollow laugh.

Powers hung up the phone, feeling like he'd just walked through the dung heap at a feed lot in his native Texas. He hated moments like these, when his agency was compromised for political reasons, but he knew he couldn't turn down a U.S. senator.

A moment later, Emily entered, shook his hand and took a seat across from him at his desk.

"You watched *The World Today* segment this morning?' he asked.

"Yes, sir."

He handed her a flash drive and a folder of files.

"Kaveri Miller Browne was found several months ago, and the news broke publicly today. The bureau investigated her disappearance before either of us were here. I have all the internal files from that investigation on the flash drive and any supplementary information I found. We've been asked to look into her reappearance to validate her identity," Powers said.

"But on the news segment they said they'd done a DNA test," Emily said, shifting uncomfortably in her chair. She held the files gingerly, as if they were hot to the touch.

"Yes, and evidently it's a match," Powers replied.

"Who's requesting that we investigate? If the family is going public with a DNA match?"

Powers paused. "It's a personal request from Senator Harry

Hubbard. We need to check out the fellow who found her. Rawley Jaynes. He worked her original abduction case. We want to be sure he's legit."

"Okay, I'm on it today," Emily said.

"This is very under wraps; I know I can rely on your discretion. You can choose an agent to work with you on this," Powers replied.

Emily fell silent for a moment before clearing her throat to speak. "Agent Andy Ryan."

"You sure? Ryan is new, just out of Quantico. You don't want a more seasoned partner on this?"

"He worked with me on the Josie Vance case when he was a detective. He's smart and driven. We have a good rapport, I think he'll do an excellent job," Emily replied. She spoke confidently, looking Powers square in the eyes, but there was something in her eagerness to get out of his office that he noted. He'd expected more questions from her, but he could sense her impatience to retreat.

"Okay, Agent Ryan it is. You'll have an office on the fifth floor at the end of the hall."

"Thank you, sir. I'll start right away," Emily said, turning to go.

As she reached the door, Powers added, "And one more thing. Find out why Senator Hubbard is so concerned about this."

The guard at the security kiosk of the Doucette-Browne compound called Mackenzie to announce Jaynes' arrival. Rawley Jaynes was always on time. And in time. He had never let her down in the many years of their acquaintance, even if she found his boorish manners and pushy personality grating. He had been there when Connor was arrested for a third drug offense and faced serious jail time. Jaynes was a vice detective in those days. He'd hidden things that could've caused a lot of trouble for her precious son.

He was acquainted with Connor's dealer, Ty Leeds, who was found beaten to death behind an empty house near Echo Park. When attention turned to Connor, Jaynes had assured Mackenzie that Leeds' death would not be investigated aggressively; no one wanted to waste taxpayer money on justice for a bottom-feeding drug dealer. Jaynes had been right about that. He'd told her to trust him, and she had. Not that it made much of a difference, Connor was found dead a month later, his lifeless body sprawled in a dirty room of the Cecil Hotel. She had called Jaynes, and he had been the first on the scene.

But today, Jaynes was delivering the piece of paper that was worth more than her stock portfolio. It was the hard copy result of Kaveri's DNA test to prove that she was Sierra's daughter, to anyone who cared to ask. She looked out the paned window of her sitting room and saw Jaynes' classic black Porsche pull up. He stepped out and she marveled at his resemblance to Food Network star, Guy Fieri. They could've been twin brothers. She opened the door with a smile.

"Hello, Rawley! It was a great day. Can I offer you something?"

"A whiskey sour would be nice," he said, giving her an air kiss before walking past her into the sitting room. She followed him with her eyes, as gray and immutable as river rock. He was reliable but he always pushed just a little too far, acting as if he were the host in her grand home, rather than the unlikely guest. She rang for the valet to order his drink. He sat on her couch covered in imported silk, his belly spilling over his belt, arms outstretched. He set a plain manila folder on the coffee table.

"It's quite a big day, Mack. A very big, big day!" he said, jovially.

She hated being called "Mack" but she smiled and deftly picked up the file. She moved to her desk and put it inside a drawer, locking it securely.

"A big day, indeed. I thought the show went very well. Not a single misstep," she agreed.

"It's going to be amazing. The exposure will be a windfall for my new venture. Zanie said we had a ton of inquiries through the website, just on the ride back from the studio!" he said.

"How is Zanie?" Mackenzie asked, barely hiding her distaste. She abhorred women like Zanie Lichtman, overreaching little climbers, desperately trying to worm their way up the social ladder.

"She's great. Got really good ideas for the new biz, good at details."

"You've carved out quite a new career for yourself, Rawley. I'm not surprised, you've always been so good at digging things up, like a hunting dog," she said.

"There are a lot of missing people out there, hoping and praying to be found," he said with a chuckle that sounded more like gargling.

"And a lot of desperate families. But luckily, we can now be taken off that list!" Mackenzie said, taking the cocktail from her maid and handing it to Jaynes.

"How's Sierra doing with all of it?" he asked.

"Struggling. She can't manage changes well."

"But Jinx knows, right?"

"Of course he knows. I told him immediately, as soon as the DNA was confirmed. I sent the digital copy to the lawyers."

"You've got two versions in the folder I brought," Jaynes said with a smile, draining his drink and setting it on the glass tabletop, despite the pile of Degás coasters. "I was hoping to catch up with Sierra. Could we call her?"

Mackenzie shook her head. "No. All of this is too much for her. She's always been fragile, you know."

She didn't like the way Jaynes always tried to get close to Sierra. Her daughter was still beautiful at thirty-five, although she'd lost the luminescence she'd had as a young woman. She'd seen the way he flirted with Sierra over the years, as if he had special privileges. The sheer audacity of his overreaching appalled her, but she had learned to keep Sierra far away from Jaynes when he came around. She had what she needed, and he'd finished his drink, so she rang a small silver bell for her personal maid, Luisa. It was the signal that she wanted to end the social engagement. Luisa knew to come in and tell her she was needed elsewhere. A moment later, Luisa arrived.

"Mr. Jinx wants to see you at the big house, ma'am," she said dutifully.

Mackenzie stood up, the signal for Jaynes to leave. "So sorry we can't visit longer, Rawley. But when the big dog barks, one must answer," she said, with a smile.

He took her hand and gave it a gallant kiss, before leaving. She watched him go from the doorway. As soon as he was out of sight, she wiped the back of her hand on her white linen pants and retreated to her home office to plan the annual gala fundraiser for the Los Angeles Opera.

Sierra Miller Browne pressed her ear to the door, listening for her mother's footsteps as she disappeared down the long hallway, then emerged from one of the extra bedrooms at the top of the stairs. Mackenzie hadn't noticed her when she came in, several hours earlier. Sierra had timed it perfectly, as she always did. Mackenzie had been distracted by the taping of the television show with Kaveri. The house was so big, no one bothered to check the perfectly appointed but unused bedrooms, not even the housekeepers who dutifully cleaned them once a week.

Sierra had favorite hiding spots all over the house. She listened in, on visitors and phone calls. That was the only way she would really know what was going on since Mackenzie kept her in the dark about most things. Like the sudden arrival of her daughter, Kaveri, whom she only had vague memories of as a baby. Recollections that made her stomach tighten up and showed up in her dreams like banshees, flitting erratically across her slumber. Kaveri was back but she seemed like a stranger to Sierra, who had long ago given up any hope of finding her. She looked at Kaveri's open expression, her wide innocent smile, and it was hard for Sierra to accept that the living, breathing young woman in front of her was her missing daughter. It seemed impossible and it unsettled her.

Sierra padded silently down the stairs and tried the drawer to the desk in the sunroom. Beams of light poured in through the windows, giving the room a warm, cozy glow. Despite the inviting sense of repose that the room evoked, she was on edge; she had to be careful not to be seen by any of the staff. Or the security cameras. She tried the desk drawer; she'd heard her mother open it when Rawley Jaynes was there but now it was locked tight. She knelt down and looked closely at the lock, jiggling the drawer again. She heard footsteps approaching and she slipped out the main door, hurrying back to her own house, across the quadrangle of the compound. Whatever her mother had hidden in that locked drawer held the answer to Kaveri's return.

SIX

Brittney Hoard sat in her trailer packing up boxes of her belongings. She had watched *The World Today* earlier, to see the daughter she had raised as Megan Hoard, sitting beside Mackenzie Miller Browne, her newfound grandmother. She still wasn't used to calling Megan by the name Kaveri, it sounded so foreign and strange. What kind of name was that anyway? It sure wasn't American.

Megan looked good on the show, wearing nice, expensive clothes, and her hair was well-tended, thick and shiny. She looked so pretty with professional makeup. Brittney owed Rawley Jaynes a call, to make sure she would be getting her next check on time. She had to pay the guys who were moving her into her new modular home across town, at the Tropicana Manufactured Home Park. She had to pay the space rental fee also. Frink wasn't really a town, it was just a blip of a neighborhood near the Salton Sea, but it was where she had lived her whole life.

She was on a stepladder getting some photos off a shelf when the front door opened and Megan's best friend, Trina Eagan, walked in. No one in the trailer park ever knocked, they just came in like it was their own home.

"Hey, Brit! Did you see Meg on that TV show?" Trina asked.

"Sure did. She looked nice. I can't believe she was on TV."

"I can't believe that she's really that girl they say she is! How did that happen? Like she's Cinderella or something!" Trina exclaimed, excitedly.

Brittney didn't answer; she knew Trina was too young to understand that Brittney's nephew and his girlfriend had showed up one day with a green-eyed baby girl and asked her to take care of her while they traveled to Thailand – and never came back. That was what she'd told Megan when Rawley Jaynes tracked her down and explained how Megan might really be Kaveri Miller Browne. Megan had been stunned to learn that Brittney wasn't her real mother but that would pass. After all, they had never had a close relationship. She'd had Megan removed from her home a few times and put into foster care. The girl only came back when she aged out of the system and had nowhere to go.

"Didn't you freak out when that private detective guy showed up?" Trina asked, sitting on a kitchen barstool and taking an apple from the countertop.

"Sure. No one expected that," Brittney said, busy with stuffing boxes.

"I Just don't get it at all. How could Meg have been living out here in bumfuck all these years? And she never knew she was as rich as shit and an heiress?"

"Well, for fuck's sake, Trina, you're only eighteen! There's a lot of stuff you don't understand, okay? Some things are for grown-ups, alright? You don't need to be worrying about what's done, got it?" Brittney snapped at her.

Trina didn't flinch. She fixed Brittney with a flat stare and said, "I was just wondering, that's all."

"Then stop wondering and help me pack up if you're going to sit there doing nothing!"

Trina jumped off the barstool. "I can't. I've got to get to work at the Circle K. I wanted to see if you saw the show, that's all."

She sauntered out the door and let it slam shut behind her. Brittney watched her go, her palms sweating. She couldn't wait to move to the Tropicana Park where visitors would have to punch in a code to get inside the security gate. She wouldn't be giving it to Trina Eagan.

SEVEN

Emily and Andy Ryan stood in front of the whiteboard in their out-of-the-way office in the federal building. They'd printed out all the information on the flash drive that Powers had given her and now the board was filled with photos and notes related to Kaveri Miller Browne's disappearance and sudden re-emergence. Stephanie Leedom, a young FBI data analyst from the CARD team, was helping them with the initial background checks.

"So, are we looking for some kind of fraud in this?" Andy asked. "If the DNA is confirmed, what's the issue?" he asked.

"It's a personal request from Senator Harry Hubbard. There's something bigger at stake. It's about a lot of money or covering up something damaging to someone's power and position," Emily replied.

"How do you know that?"

"With people this rich, it's always about money. Or something that money can't fix."

"So, we talk to the family first, right?" he asked.

"Right. But we have to dig into all of these family members, so we're armed with all the information before we meet with Mackenzie Miller Browne. She's not going to be happy to see us, and she'll be ready with her arsenal of lawyers and publicists to spin whatever this is in her favor."

"Do you think the old guy, this Jinx Doucette-Browne is going to be able to talk to us? He's ninety years old," Ryan asked, skeptically. "And Mackenzie is the only one of his kids still alive? What the hell? Suicide, overdose. What a mess," he grumbled, scanning through the family history.

"The oldest son and namesake, called J.J., drove his motorcycle off a cliff in Carmel at the age of twenty-six, under the influence of a hallucinogenic cocktail," Stephanie chimed in. "There was speculation that it might have been suicide but that was quickly quashed by the family. Jinx took out hefty life insurance policies on all of his kids at birth and suicide would have made them null and void."

"Nice. Make money when your kid dies before you," Ryan said, dryly.

Stephanie continued. "The next sibling, Carmela, was the only one who died naturally, of an illness that her father's money couldn't cure. Acute myeloid leukemia at twenty-two. By all accounts, Jinx went kind of crazy after that. In the ten years that followed, the second son, Jasper Doucette-Browne overdosed in a New Orleans hotel room and Emmeline Amaya Doucette-Browne took her own life, at her home in Montecito. Her young daughter, Laurel, had died in a freak accident the year prior. Kaveri is the only surviving grandchild. So, Kaveri is the only heir, outside of Mackenzie Miller Browne and her daughter, Sierra," Stephanie said with finality.

"Anyone else? Anyone who stands to gain when Jinx dies?" Ryan asked.

"Not anything obvious. I'd have to get into the trust documents to find out for sure. I imagine there are charities and other entities that are getting large donations to their endowments. It's all handled by City National Bank and they have a pretty thick firewall to protect their high-value clients. I still have to do the rundown on Rawley Jaynes, who is now a private investigator. And I have a couple of high priority cases as well," Stephanie said.

"Anything else of importance?" Emily asked.

"The whole Doucette-Browne family are deeply involved in various charities and philanthropic organizations, and Jinx has serious political connections in Washington. His companies have poured millions into campaign coffers. He has an especially close connection to Senator Harry Hubbard, a fraternity brother from their time at Texas A&M."

"How close is close?" Ryan asked.

"Close enough that Jinx has made huge contributions to his campaigns and other special projects," Stephanie said.

"Which means into his pockets, basically," Emily added.

Then Stephanie said, "I'm compiling the information on Rawley Jaynes and I'm about to dive into Mackenzie and Sierra next."

"Thanks, Steph. Ryan and I will start reaching out to Jaynes' former colleagues in the LAPD and the FBI agents who worked Kaveri's disappearance. We'll have everything in order when we head over to speak to Mackenzie Miller Browne," Emily said, scanning the Jaynes file.

"Can we just call them the Brownes? I can't deal with having to say all those names every time," Ryan asked, suddenly, his brown eyes wide.

Emily smiled. Ryan was as authentic and unpretentious as a man could be, and she liked that about him.

"Of course, let's just call them the Brownes," she agreed, with a laugh.

"Look, you can take the boy out of Redondo Beach, but you can't take Redondo Beach out of the boy. They live in Holmby Hills; where is that exactly?" he asked.

"It's an area in Beverly Hills, super-rich, super-exclusive. The homes have guard kiosks and that type of thing. A lot of venture capitalists. I hear the Browne compound sits on ten acres."

Ryan whistled. "Ten acres in Beverly Hills? That's a shit load of money!"

"Most of it dirty, I bet," Emily added. "This Rawley Jaynes guy doesn't seem like a boy scout, either. Check out his LAPD history. He was let go from the department for unprofessional conduct." She handed him Jaynes' LAPD file.

"So, he framed suspects or stole evidence, or some other illegal stuff. We can put him in the bad player category," Ryan said.

Emily's phone rang and she saw the call was from Larissa Cinque, the young reporter who had covered the Josie Vance case earlier in the year. Larissa had moved up from a small, South Bay newspaper called *The Daily Breeze* to the *Los Angeles Times*.

"Hello, Larissa, nice to hear from you,' Emily said warmly.

"You too, Emily. I wanted to know if you caught the news story this morning about Kaveri Miller Browne?" Larissa asked.

"Yes, I did. It was very—"

Larissa cut her off mid-sentence, "And did you see that the detective found Danica Hansen? Do you remember her? I did a story about her disappearance during the Josie Vance case. She was kidnapped a couple of years after you were!" Larissa's excitement spilled over as her words ran together.

"Yes, I remember her case quite well," Emily said, trying to keep her voice and facial expression neutral.

"So, I asked my editor if I could do a follow-up story with Danica now that she's been located. I've already got an interview booked with her real family out in the South Bay. Remember when we went to her aunt Janelle's place and spoke to her?"

Emily nodded, acutely aware of Ryan and Stephanie watching and waiting for her.

"I remember that."

"I wanted to know if you'd like to go with me to talk to them again? Her mother, Amber, will be there this time. I'd really appreciate your take on them. I felt there was something off about Danica on that news segment. Like she really didn't want to be there."

Emily paused, considering the emotional toll the visit would take on her, but knowing that it was an invaluable opportunity to gain insight into how Rawley Jaynes worked.

"Sure, I'd be happy to accompany you. Just send me the details, I'll meet you there."

Emily hung up and turned to Ryan and Stephanie. "Larissa Cinque is meeting with Danica Hansen's biological family to discuss how she was found, and she's invited me to go along with her."

"That's great! You can ask them how it all went down. Rawley Jaynes said that there was a DNA match in that case as well," Ryan said.

Emily knew that there had to be a compelling reason for Amber and Janelle to go along with the fraud of Danica's reappearance. She was very curious to learn exactly how her mother had confirmed that a stranger's DNA was a match to hers. And how the daughter she'd never bothered to look for had, miraculously, been found alive.

EIGHT

Kaveri walked through Beverly Connection Mall with Gerte, who looked like a nurse with her severe gray bob haircut and a traditional maid's uniform. Gerte wanted her to go to the fancy stores in Beverly Hills, on Rodeo Drive, the ones Mackenzie had suggested earlier. Those were the only places that the granddaughter of Mr. Jinx should be seen, she'd said, not the local mall where anyone could come and go, without spending any money. Kaveri remembered doing just that with her best friend from home, Trina, at the Imperial Mall when all they could afford was a shared Wetzel's Pretzel.

Kaveri had tried the high-end stores a few weeks earlier, but she was uncomfortable with the way the clerks looked at her, like she didn't belong there. It had made shopping tense and uncomfortable and today, she just wanted to enjoy herself. Mackenzie had drilled into her head that the appearance on *The World Today* was of the utmost importance, it was her formal, public introduction to the world she now belonged to.

The whole thing was like a Disney movie. She'd been working at a coffee shop in Frink, near the Salton Sea. She was like the girls she saw working in the mall kiosks, in the fast-food court. Just a girl trying to stay above water until she could move out of Brittney's place. Then Mr. Jaynes arrived and started talking to her about how she was kidnapped by someone and ended up with Brittney, who wasn't her real mother. She looked at the people working at TJ Maxx, the mall security guard strolling up and down the brightly lit walkways. That would have been her life, but it had all changed in an instant.

At twenty, she was the heir to a huge fortune that belonged to the old, withered man she had met a few times since she'd arrived at the compound. They called him Jinx. Sierra Miller Browne was her real mother and Mackenzie was her grandmother. She could order Door Dash every night; she had already bought a ton of new electronics and fancy makeup from Sephora. Today's shopping trip was a reward for the appearance on television.

Mackenzie had been prepping her for weeks, rehearsing how she would tell her story, reinforcing the details that Kaveri didn't remember from her early childhood. She'd had to learn how to sit properly, with her legs crossed at the ankles. Mackenzie had coached her on speaking clearly, explaining that Kaveri's flat, vocal fry sounded common. Kaveri had never used the word common the way Mackenzie did. She thought "common" meant shared, but evidently, it meant low class. Now, Kaveri heard it everywhere and it made her cringe.

Kaveri's phone rang just as she was taking a dress off the rack in TJ Maxx.

"Hello?"

The voice of her best friend answered, bubbling with excitement. "Meg! It's me, Trina!"

"Hey! You can't call me that anymore! My grandmother gets mad, and I have a handler keeping an eye on me," Kaveri said, moving away from Gerte.

"You mean the Nazi one called Gerte?" Trina teased.

Kaveri couldn't help but crack a smile. "Yes, that one. She'll lose it if she hears you."

"I saw you on the news today, You looked great! Your shoes were fire! I went by your mom's – she watched it too."

"How is Brittney?"

"Seemed cool. She's packing 'cause she bought one of those manufactured homes in a new area called the Tropicana Park. It's luxe, each house has its own jacuzzi!" Trina said.

"She can't afford something like that! Where'd she get the money?" Kaveri asked, her brow furrowed in suspicion.

"I don't know. She's got a new boyfriend, too. He's a trucker named Kevin."

"At least this one has a job."

"So, when are you inviting me up to your new house?" Trina asked.

Kaveri looked at her shopping cart, piled high with new outfits to try on. At home she had a new MacBook Pro, the latest iPhone 16 Pro Max, Xbox and a PlayStation. She knew Trina would faint when she saw the compound and learned that Kaveri would get to choose one of the big empty houses all for herself. She suddenly felt embarrassed and self-conscious. She knew Mackenzie would make Trina feel like a strange zoo animal who had wandered into the wrong habitat.

"In a few weeks, when things settle down a little," Kaveri lied. She missed Trina and just hanging out, doing nothing together. But her life had changed, everything had to be planned and precise now. She remembered Mackenzie's words earlier that day.

People only want to get close to use you, blackmail you, and get money out of you... you'll learn in time...

As Trina chattered on about life in Frink, Kaveri began to realize all the things she would have to give up.

Senator Harry Hubbard signaled the waiter at Bistro Cacao for a refill of his Scotch, even if it was only midday. He waved to several of his colleagues across the room; this was a favorite of senators on his side of the aisle. His salade aux crevettes was excellent and he was waiting on the trout Amandine, his favorite from the lunch menu.

He dined alone today; he was expecting a phone call that he couldn't risk having anyone else overhear. He'd watched *The World Today* segment with Mackenzie and Kaveri Browne and he had to admit, the girl bore a strong resemblance to Sierra. He hadn't seen Sierra in a decade; for years she'd been absent from the holiday parties that Jinx hosted.

He'd had the communications staff in his office find information on the FBI agents who were handling his inquiry into Kaveri Browne. Special Agent Emily Ray was quite impressive, having survived being kidnapped as a child and returning to become a high-level federal agent. Andrew Ryan was a new agent, quite good-looking from his FBI photo, Hubbard thought. The waiter arrived with a refill of his drink and Hubbard took a sip. He felt confident that things would work out in his favor.

After all, Mackenzie and Sierra all had their own big trust funds that Jinx had established years ago. His estate would simply pour even more money into their large personal coffers. They didn't need the extra funds, not the way he did. And all the years of loyalty, covering up Jinx's dirty business deals and pushing legislation that was advantageous to him and his fellow one percenters was worth something more than a house on Grand Cayman to go with his offshore account.

He hadn't had a chance to speak to Jinx personally for some months; the old man's health was rapidly deteriorating. He'd spoken to Gerte, "his loyal handmaid", as she was known to his inner circle of cohorts. She didn't have much to say, always the same stoic replies and formal explanations. She was never one who was up for fun; he remembered that about her.

Mackenzie had stopped returning his calls several years earlier; he figured that she resented the changes her father had made in his will. Hubbard didn't care what she thought; Jinx was the one he had to maintain ties with. His phone rang and he answered it immediately. The voice on the other end was deep and distorted, the speaker was clearly using a device to protect his identity. He called himself Uriel, like the arch angel who oversees Tartarus, the place of punishment for fallen angels. The congruity of his situation was not lost on Hubbard.

"Senator?" Uriel asked.

"Yes, this is me. I'm here," Harry replied, dabbing the faint sheen of perspiration from his upper lip.

"How are things proceeding?"

"Just fine. I expect to have the money you requested within the next quarter. I'm waiting for settlement that should be coming through," Hubbard explained.

"I don't care where you get the money, that's your business. Just be sure it is delivered in full by the date we agreed upon. Or we'll release everything we have to the press."

Hubbard grimaced, his face tight with fury, but he kept his tone civil and friendly.

"Oh, yes. That is understood. And you confirm the destruction of the original source material. We agreed this would not be an ongoing negotiation after the money is delivered," Hubbard said.

"Agreed. Just know that if you are late with the money, the photos, the videos, the text messages, all of it gets leaked to all major news outlets. The boy still isn't yet eighteen so there would be serious consequences for you, Senator," Uriel said, enjoying the clear and unseemly menace in these details.

"Understood, thank you."

Hubbard hung up the phone, his hands trembling. He wished he could reach through the phone line and strangle the life out of that thug on the other end, the negotiator, or whoever had managed to get ahold of the incriminating evidence. He knew it was more than a leak in his office or on the Hill. Whoever had acquired the evidence was accustomed to playing on a much bigger field and his usual intimidation tactics weren't going to work.

It used to be so easy, before the internet, before camera phones. In the days when people couldn't get their hands on everything, when there were no cell towers to be tracked, no video footage at their fingertips. He used to be able to do whatever he wanted at the discreet Pearl Hotel. The staff were compliant, understanding the position and power of men like him in Washington. He'd had set-ups like that his whole life, starting in college, and he'd never had any real issues until recently. Yes, there were a couple of trouble-makers over the years, but he'd been able to silence them one way or another.

But this time was different; the threats against him were beyond the scope of his power and influence; he would go to prison if they were exposed. The waiter arrived with his trout and set the plate in front of him on the white linen tablecloth.

"Here you are, Senator, just the way you like it."

"Thank you," he said, adjusting the plate and brushing his fingers against the back of the young man's hand.

The fish was perfect; tender and flaky under his fork. He'd check in with his buddy John Powers in the next day or so. The investigation into Kaveri Browne shouldn't take long. He'd have the answer he was hoping for soon and then the whole thing would be over. If Jinx kicked the bucket sooner rather than later, he'd even be able to close the deal before the due date.

NINE

Emily and Andy Ryan sat across from one another in their office, poring over the information they'd gathered to build a profile of all the players in the Kaveri Browne case. Since their office was out of the way and the investigation wasn't a standard, by-the-book case, Ryan had removed his suit jacket and rolled up his shirtsleeves as he assessed the material they had so far. Emily watched him for a moment, his boyish appearance at odds with his laser-like focus on the task at hand. She noticed, for the first time, that he had dimples.

"You look like the lead actor in a rom-com. When the two characters who hate each other have to work late and then they get sparky," she said with a grin.

"Sparky? Did you make that word up?" he laughed.

"No. Well, sort of. But you know how those movies are. The stiff, button-down guy lets loose and then there's chemistry," she explained.

"Are you hitting on me, Agent Ray?" he asked with a wink.

"Of course not! I'm married and you're gay!" she protested.

"Yeah, there's that. But I could be sparky, you know!"

"Shut up!" she said, swatting him with a file. "Forget I said it, back to work!"

Stephanie had delivered the background search on Mackenzie and Sierra as well as Rawley Jaynes. Emily stared at a handful of photos. At twenty, Kaveri had dark golden hair and green eyes, with straight, even teeth. She was tall and slender, like her mother, Sierra.

"This abduction doesn't make sense," Ryan said, with an exasperated sigh. "How did someone get into a compound like that? It had to be someone on the inside."

"I agree. But no ransom demand is even weirder. Why take a wealthy heiress if you don't want money?" Emily mused.

"Maybe it's a family member who set it up. Who doesn't want to split the inheritance?" Ryan asked.

"There are only three of them, the grandmother, the mother and Kaveri. Maybe if it were a sibling, but it's hard to imagine Sierra or Mackenzie doing it. They all have more than they'll ever be able to spend."

"Money makes people do strange things sometimes," Ryan said.

Emily made a list of all the people who worked within the compound, former and current, who were present the day of the kidnapping. It included the staff inside the houses: maids, cooks, assistants and valets. Many had died or moved away. The outdoor staff was made up of full-time groundskeepers, a pool man, an electrician, a computer technician and the security team. The groundskeeping foreman, Johan Kaspar, was still working for the family as was the senior housekeeper, Gerte Brose.

"We have a lot of people to talk to. The staff at the Doucette-Browne home at that time. If they are still there or have financial ties to the family, there will be pushback. Let's start with the former FBI agents involved in Kaveri's case and the cops. And I'm curious to find out how Rawley Jaynes followed a thread to Kaveri that paid off after all these years," Emily said.

"This must be weird for you..." Ryan's voice trailed off. He was looking at her intensely and she felt her cheeks color. "I know you've been through it yourself."

She coughed nervously. The last thing she wanted was speculation about her own history but Ryan had hit her emotional bull's eye. She felt like there was a target embossed on her chest, drawing everyone's attention to the similarities between her and Kaveri Browne.

"I've been there so I understand how it can happen," she replied evenly.

Becoming Emily Ray had defined her life and brought solace to her father, Michael Ray. It was as if she had kept Emily alive, for herself as much as for him. She had lived with that weight a long time; it was a part of her now. But the secret that she had guarded her entire adult life loomed heavily over her as she delved into the background of young Kaveri Browne.

"What a mess. I feel bad for the girl, stepping into this shitstorm," Ryan muttered, as he turned back to the whiteboard.

"Me, too," Emily agreed. She hoped Kaveri Miller Browne was legit; she didn't want to imagine the kind of nightmare the girl would face if she were exposed as a fraud. Emily felt a sudden spasm run up her spine; it was the fear she had lived with daily for twenty-three years. She gave Ryan a list of names and numbers.

"You start with Jaynes' colleagues in the LAPD, I'll call the FBI agents who handled the case," Emily said, hoping she could quiet the thoughts that kept running through her head.

What if they had looked into you the same way? What if they knew the truth? What if... what if...

Half an hour later, Emily waited on the phone for Sam Cole, a retired FBI agent who had worked the Kaveri Browne abduction eighteen years earlier, while Ryan chatted away with Rawley Jaynes' former partner at the LAPD. Stephanie's deep dive into Mackenzie and Sierra had not yielded anything suspect or significant. They'd both lived privileged, protected lives with the Browne fortune and connections to provide a large safety net. Sierra had battled a drug problem since her teens, been to rehab multiple times and Mackenzie divorced her stockbroker husband years ago and never remarried. Emily was reading through their information when she heard Sam Cole's voice come on the line.

"Special Agent Cole? This is Special Agent Emily Ray from the Los Angeles office. I wanted to reach out to you about the Kaveri Browne investigation," she said.

Sam Cole's voice was warm and deep. "You can call me Sam. I'm long retired now. I saw that the girl's been found after all these years. By the detective who worked that case, that Jaynes fellow."

"We've been asked to look into this reappearance, and I wanted to hear your thoughts about the whole thing. Rawley Jaynes, how the investigation went."

Sam Cole paused, then said, "It was strange right from the get-go. The mother, Sierra, was a mess. Drugged out on cocaine and who knows what else. A real pretty girl, too. Just barely nineteen. But all the Doucette-Browne kids were screwed up. Sierra had the little girl with some guy she'd met out in Oregon, when she was living on a farm run by a con man named Kandar Steinberg, a kind of guru type. She'd come back to the family compound, tried rehab and had the little girl with her. She was passed out when Kaveri disappeared, didn't remember a thing."

"The file says Sierra was poolside with Kaveri. There were no other family members or staff present?"

"Didn't seem that way. I always thought it was weird. Who leaves a toddler by a pool with someone who's knocked out on drugs? But a lot of things were strange about that case."

"What was strange about it?" Emily asked, taking notes.

Sam paused, searching for the right words to say. "It was like the family didn't really want to work with us, not after the first push. You'd think they'd be on our backs, turning over every rock to find her but after the first few weeks, they shut down and circled the wagons. They gave us basic information; it had to be some kind of inside job, with all that security. We only spoke to Sierra twice before they sent her away to another closed rehab center in Brazil."

It was clear to Emily that he still struggled with the memory of the investigation, the sense that he could have done more.

He continued. "I got the feeling that the scandal was the worst thing for them. Mackenzie didn't want any talk or speculation after all the problems they had. The messy divorces, the drug overdoses. She wanted to present an image that was whitewashed of all the bad stuff. Mackenzie wanted the uproar to go away quickly, that was her priority."

"What about Jinx? How did he react?"

"He was upset for a little while, he's the one who called us in. You know, he has connections. He was a mean son of a bitch, you could tell. All the kids were scared of him. To me, it felt the little girl mattered because she was part of his portfolio, you know? Like someone had stolen his stocks and he wanted what was his returned. But even he lost interest after a while."

"Did he have any solid information? Any suspicions?"

"He had plenty of suspicions. He thought it was the Russians, or left-wing radicals, all nonsense. None of that panned out. He was worked up about someone targeting him. The only heirs left are Mackenzie, Sierra and Kaveri. That's a hell of a lot of money for just three people!" Sam said, with a dry laugh.

"What about Rawley Jaynes?"

Sam sighed. "I never liked that guy. He was dirty, you could tell a mile away. He'd been the first one out there, it seemed. The family had called it in, and he showed up with his partner, Ken Carlisle. They resented us, like they do sometimes. He was all bluster, made a lot of noise. But he couldn't find anything either. The security guards were terrified, they hadn't seen anyone or anything strange. Nothing was on the camera footage, it looked like whoever did it had somehow evaded the system. I remember there was a gap in the video, it jumped from one spot to another and that had to have been when she was taken. But they never found out who it was."

"So, someone had access to the security footage?"

"They had to, but trying to get those staff people to talk was like getting blood from a turnip. Stone-faced, cold as ice. Loyal to the old man."

"Thank you, Sam, I'll circle back around if I need anything else," Emily said.

"I'll do the same if I remember any new details. But the case file has everything."

Emily hung up, frustrated. They were charged with verifying Kaveri Browne's identity, but she wanted a broader perspective on her disappearance. Sam Cole was right; it was strange that Mackenzie Browne had not been more concerned about her granddaughter's disappearance. Emily had years of experience working with families of missing kids, they were usually overwrought and terrified, pushing constantly for answers. She drew a red circle around Mackenzie's name. Ryan joined her in perusing the information they'd gathered so far.

"Jaynes' patrol partner said he's a blow-hard attention hound. Always wanting to take the credit for everything," he said, shaking his head. "And Jaynes had a lot of complaints against him for misconduct. The guy I spoke to only worked with him as a street cop. When Jaynes moved on to the detective division, he teamed up with Ken Carlisle. Carlisle's still at Rampart. I didn't leave a message."

"Good, we have time to get over there today and surprise him. He might be able to fill us in on the history Jaynes has with the Browne family," Emily said.

"What do we have on Danica Hansen?" Ryan asked, eagerly. "I really want to find out her story."

"I'll find out more tomorrow morning when I meet her real family with Larissa. But she's a fraud," Emily said, her disdain obvious.

Ryan stared at her for a surprised beat. "How do you know for sure?"

Emily looked up at him, flustered. "I don't... know for certain. It's just a gut instinct I have."

"Want me to go with you when you meet them?" he offered.

"No, it might intimidate them to see two of us. There's plenty you can do to prepare for visiting Mackenzie Browne. We'll go as soon as I get back from the South Bay."

"Should we call Mackenzie first? Let her know we're coming tomorrow?" Ryan asked.

Emily looked at him coolly, and said, "I don't think so."

TEN

Sierra Miller Browne pulled back the filmy curtains of her bedroom window and watched as her mother, Mackenzie, stood in the driveway, greeting Kaveri who had returned from shopping with Gerte. Several maids carried the bags and boxes inside. Sierra's house was kitty corner to Mackenzie's off the main quadrangle of the Doucette-Browne compound. Her grandfather, Jinx, had designed it this way so that everyone faced a central point, as if to remind them that they had to remain within the gravitational pull of the family and his influence.

She felt a pang of jealousy that her mother had taken over Kaveri's return to them, how she fawned over the girl and lavished expensive gifts on her. Sierra flinched when she saw how Mackenzie smoothed a piece of Kaveri's hair into place. She didn't want that attention for herself; she wondered what Mackenzie's end game was with her daughter, because she knew there had to be one. She felt an instinctive shudder of fear for Kaveri when she saw Mackenzie drawing her near.

Sierra struggled to remember life before her daughter's disappearance. She had been so young, barely eighteen when Kaveri was born. Security officers hired by her mother and grandfather had taken her and baby Kaveri from the farm in Oregon that she had run away to. She loved living on Kandar's Farm, with other young people, in a communal setting. She'd had friends who didn't even know that she was an heiress, who didn't care about her bank account or inheritance. Baby Kaveri had other children her age to play with, and farm animals and open fields of wild blackberries to pick.

Now, she watched her grown daughter from the window, unloading her packages and chatting effusively with Mackenzie. Sierra wondered what their lives would've been like if Mackenzie and Jinx hadn't interfered, dragging them back to the family compound.

Would Kaveri have been kidnapped? Or would she have grown up in the orchards and the fields, with the gray cloud cover and cool rain that kept Oregon green and lush all year. Would she have been an earth child, with her mother, living peacefully, away from the machinations of the Doucette-Browne legacy that weighed so heavily on Sierra's shoulders? For herself, Sierra liked to believe that she might not have spent so many years in and out of rehab, battling one pharmaceutical coping mechanism after another, while living yoked to her mother and family.

Sierra gripped the filmy curtain in her fingers, wanting desperately to run down to the driveway and take Kaveri's hand, to have her daughter model her new clothes, to do the simple things that mothers and daughters did every day. She wasn't sure what to say to the girl, what questions to ask but Sierra had spent her life unsure where to step next, what road to follow, who to believe. Her inner compass was so fragile and unsteady; she had never learned to trust herself. Mackenzie had always treated Sierra as if she were a liability, an unreliable element in the carefully curated mythology of the Doucette-Browne family.

Now, Sierra had the unsettling sense that she must overcome her fears and insecurities. The moment had come for her to step up and be a mother to her daughter, for the first time in her life.

. . .

Emily and Ryan pulled up outside the Rampart Division, which served the communities adjacent to downtown Los Angeles. Rawley Jaynes had worked there for years as a detective, and they wanted to speak to Ken Carlisle and any other colleagues of Jaynes who still remained. They walked in and introduced themselves to the officer manning the reception desk. He was a young cop with a marine haircut and a baby face; Ryan guessed that he probably had to shave only twice a week.

"Let me see if Detective Carlisle is available. He might be out in the field," the young cop said, dialing an extension on his desk phone. "Detective? There are two FBI special agents here to see you, Emily Ray and Andy Ryan."

A moment later, Ken Carlisle emerged from the inner offices where the detective division was located. He was tall and gaunt, his blue eyes faded and careworn. He gave the overall impression of a man who had seen too much and hoped to forget the memories that remained.

"Detective Ken Carlisle, what can I do for you?" He extended his hand, which Emily gripped firmly as she introduced herself.

Ryan followed suit and said, "We're looking into the Kaveri Browne case. You've probably seen that she's returned home. You and Rawley Jaynes worked that case; we just have a few questions."

Carlisle ran his hand over his eyes. Emily noted a slight slump to his shoulders when Jaynes' name was mentioned.

"Can we talk about this outside?" he asked. "I don't have a lot of time."

They followed him outside where he sat wearily on a concrete bench near the entrance to the station, next to an ash bucket for cigarette butts.

"What do you want to know?" he asked. "We worked that case for weeks, we had nothing. The Feds had nothing, your guys were on it with us."

"Did you find the family cooperative? "Emily asked.

"Yeah, in the beginning. Rawley knew them, he'd dealt with

Mackenzie's son, Connor, several times in the years before that. You know, the Ty Leeds homicide and how Connor was in hot water over that. And then when they found him dead at the Cecil, Rawley was the first one there. He and Mackenzie Browne had a history."

"We'd like to know more about that," Emily prodded. "We saw the news segment last night and they seemed quite familiar with each other. Jasmin Lourdes said that he had worked on Kaveri's abduction but you're saying it predated that?"

Now Carlisle's eyes darted back and forth between them and his energy shifted. Emily sensed he was deciding how much to reveal.

"Well, yeah. I thought you guys knew that. He became tight with Mackenzie Miller Browne back when her son started having a lot of legal trouble, you know, with the drugs and stuff."

"What was the Ty Leeds case?" Ryan asked.

Carlisle drew a pack of Marlboro cigarettes out of his jacket pocket and lit one, blowing a mouthful of smoke away from Emily and Ryan, his eyes scanning the street with practiced vigilance. He was buying time before answering.

"Leeds was a drug dealer, he sold to a lot of high-end clients on the Westside, in Beverly Hills. Connor was moving some stuff for him to a bunch of people out near Trancas in Malibu, you know celebrities' kids and that group. And he got busted 'cause he sold them some bad drugs, contaminated or cut with something lethal. A bunch of them got really sick, and they weren't street kids, you know? Their parents had money, so it got attention. Connor wasn't sharp, that kid. Too much money, not enough brain power."

"And Jaynes was involved?" Emily asked.

"Yeah. When Connor was busted in Malibu, Rawley intervened and helped out, since he'd dealt with the family in the past," Carlisle said.

"Helped out how?" Emily prodded. Carlisle looked at her with a pained expression.

"You'll have to track that down for yourselves, okay?"

"And what went down with Leeds?" Ryan asked again, circling back.

"He was found dead, in an alley off of Alvarado. They looked at all of his clients and associates."

"And Connor Browne was one of them?" Emily asked.

"Of course, he'd known Leeds for a long time. And he had a beef with him over the bad drugs. Rawley and I took the case," Carlisle said, "but nothing came of it. Then when Connor overdosed, Mackenzie called him first. He became her go-to guy for anything that could attract negative publicity. She called us when Kaveri disappeared, and we worked that case from the start."

"But why did you take it if you're way out here in Rampart and they were in Beverly Hills? The city has its own police force," Emily asked.

"I know, but it was some kind of... favor or something. I think the old man, Jinx Doucette, was involved with it. The Beverly Hills cops were on it, but we were the leads..." He paused, taking a last deep puff of his cigarette. Emily noticed a slight tremor in his fingers. He was nervous. "I got to go. We're working a case and I've probably talked too much anyway, but what the fuck, right? I'm just glad the girl is back."

"One last thing, why do you think Jaynes was able to find her now? After all these years?" Emily asked.

Carlisle sighed again and tossed his cigarette butt into the ash bucket, "I guess he found her because he had to."

Ryan drove them back to Westwood. They fell into a comfortable silence as Emily investigated the information that Carlisle had given them on her laptop.

"What do you think? About the Browne–Jaynes connection?" Ryan asked.

"I think it's hella convenient to have a detective on your payroll that can cover up the crap you don't want to come to light," Emily replied.

"I bet that's why he got fired. That stuff with Ty Leeds is bad. To me, it looks like Connor Browne killed him and Jaynes covered it up."

"I agree. We need to talk to the detectives who handled the case out in Trancas. I'd like to hear what they have to say about Jaynes helping out." Emily shifted the laptop balanced on her knees and stretched her neck. She could feel the tension creeping into her head.

"Let's go now, get everything ready for talking to Mackenzie tomorrow," Ryan suggested.

"I like your attitude, Andy. Gotta love a guy who faces things head on and gets to work!" she said with an appreciative nod.

"I learned from you, Special Agent Ray," he said with a wink, turning onto the freeway that would take them to the exclusive, northern environs of Malibu.

Gerte Brose finished hanging up the new clothes that Kaveri had picked up at the mall and pulled the curtains open in Jinx Doucette-Browne's bedroom, the afternoon sunlight spilling across the heavy Persian rug. His caretaker, Sozi, had a doctor's appointment and Gerte would take over his care, as was customary.

Sozi was the third caregiver they'd had since Mr. Jinx had deteriorated over the past two years. It was hard to find good help with the same values and loyalty that the old-time staff brought to the job. The younger staff didn't like being called servants, as if being in service were shameful.

She went through her duties as if on autopilot; so familiar were the tasks that had defined her days at the Doucette-Browne compound. She adjusted Jinx' frail hands as they clutched his blankets, fingering the edges obsessively. His hands were like popsicle sticks in her palm and she felt a pang of distress to see how far the once-powerful man had slipped away in recent years. Those hands had wielded riding crops and raised heavy crystal glasses filled with champagne. They had handed over her weekly salary and signed her travel documents from Germany when he brought her over to work for him. His cloudy eyes, once so sharp that they could pierce her heart and stop her from speaking, wandered over her face, unsure of who she was.

She pulled back his Egyptian cotton sheets and the sharp smell of ammonia hit her nostrils. He had urinated again, and this was the third mattress they would have to replace. In his stubbornness, he refused to wear a diaper, forcing the staff to clean up after him several times a day. She deftly cleaned him up and laid heavy towels over the mattress. She put him in a fresh pair of pajamas the way she would dress a doll as a child, back home in Bavaria.

He settled back onto his bed, struggling to pull himself up of his own volition. Gerte adjusted him with her strong arms and raised the bed so he could easily see the television. "Is that good, Mr. Jinx?" she asked, smiling at his gaunt face and rheumy eyes.

He nodded, patting her hand with his bony fingers.

"The show... I want to see... the show..." he whispered, gesturing toward the big screen television mounted on the wall.

"You want to see Miss Mackenzie and Miss Kaveri on the show this morning?" she asked, loudly. He nodded.

She propped him securely against the big pillow and took the remote, setting the television to replay the recorded broadcast. When Mackenzie and Kaveri appeared on screen, he leaned forward, squinting his eyes at them.

"Is that her? Kaveri?" he asked.

Gerte patted his hand reassuringly. "Yes, that's her, Mr. Jinx. She's come home now after so long."

He pushed her hand away, his frail body swaying from the effort. Gerte put out a hand to steady him.

"How... can that be... her?" he asked, his voice a hoarse croak. "How can... she be... back?"

"She was found after a long time missing. Mr. Jaynes found her and she's your great-granddaughter. Miss Sierra's daughter. You've met her, do you remember?" Gerte asked gently.

"I've met her?... Yes, I remember... I met her. But that's... not Kaveri," he said, waving his hand at the screen.

Gerte froze, her eyes trained on his face for any sign of real recognition of what he was saying.

"Yes, she is, Mr. Jinx. She's Kaveri. They did the tests to prove it, remember?"

"What tests?" he said, his voice rising. "Who... did a... test?"

"Miss Mackenzie had the tests done, to prove that she's really Miss Sierra's daughter. You just don't remember. She showed you the tests, she gave them to Mr. Rohner."

"Rohner? The lawyer? You know... how much money that... asshole stole from me?" Jinx made a feeble attempt at a shout. Gerte moved to his medicine cupboard and opened a bottle of Ativan. She took a pill to him with a glass of water.

"You can't get all worked up, you'll make yourself sick. How about I order your toast and tea from the kitchen? And some poached eggs," she suggested, handing him the sedative which he dutifully washed down. He leaned back against the pillows and gestured at the television.

"That isn't... Kaveri... Kaveri is... gone," he insisted, his voice fading.

ELEVEN

Ryan drove the scenic highway along the ocean that went from Santa Monica out to Malibu, passing the Pacific Palisades, recently torched by a raging wildfire.

"Jesus! Look at this! I haven't been out here since the fire!" He let out a deep sigh as they rolled past the scorched apocalyptic landscape.

Their car approached a security checkpoint, patrolled by uniformed police officers. Emily flashed her FBI badge. "We're investigating a case and need to speak to detectives at the Lost Hills police station."

"Go right ahead," the cop said, waving them through.

They arrived at the station and Detective Ralph Ellis stepped out to meet them – a tall, heavyset man with a fleshy face and dark eyes set a bit too far apart that gave him the appearance of being perpetually surprised.

"I'm Ralph Ellis, I understand you're from the FBI? How can I help you?"

"I'm Special Agent Emily Ray, this is Special Agent Andy Ryan. We'd like to discuss the Connor Miller Browne drug case that your division handled. It took place out in Trancas about twenty years ago? I know it's been a long time," Emily said.

Ellis frowned and shook his head. "I remember it. I'll never forget it. We had that punk dead to rights. He sold them bad shit, really bad. I don't know who his supplier was but it was bad. Several of them had to go to the hospital, the rest spent three days puking their guts out, having delusions. And the one kid, Kevin Looney, he was fucked up forever."

"We heard he suffered brain damage," Ryan said.

"More than that! He's in a wheelchair! Connor was guilty and we had him. Then we got a call that the drugs had to be transferred to the main LAPD evidence archive in L.A. And guess what? They disappeared. No drugs, no case. The asshole walked."

"How did the transfer happen?" Emily asked.

Ellis fixed them with a hard, bitter stare. "Why weren't you guys looking into this back then? Why now? Connor Miller Browne's been dead for years. Poor Kevin Looney lives with his elderly mother, last I heard. Totally dependent on her and they've spent their life savings on his care."

His anger was palpable, still ready to explode into a raging conflagration.

"I know it must be frustrating. We're looking into a different situation that involves Rawley Jaynes and we know he was helping out on the Trancas drug case," Emily said, calmly.

Now Ellis chortled. "Rawley Jaynes helped out? He's a dirtbag who I've always believed tampered with that evidence. We filed complaints against him with the California D.O.J., but nothing came of it. It's the old man's money that did it."

"You mean Jinx Doucette-Browne?" Ryan asked.

"Yeah, the old crypt keeper. It wasn't even reported much in the press. The whole thing was covered up. Alexander and I were furious about it. Jaynes was the one who came and picked up the evidence, we didn't even get to take it in personally. I still get crazy when I think about it," Ellis said.

"Thank you. We're trying to verify how far back the link between Jaynes and the Browne family extends," Emily said.

"It goes way back. By the time Connor messed up those kids at that party, Jaynes had already helped him out a bunch of times. And everyone knows he killed that dealer, the Leeds guy. Connor had been high as a kite, looking for the guy for weeks, saying he was going to take him out because of the Trancas shit show. Jaynes is their lapdog, delivers whatever they ask him for. That's the problem in the country; money can buy you any damn thing. I hated that case," Ellis said.

"Thank you for your time, Detective. We appreciate your input," Emily said.

"You want to get a real sense of what that rich kid got away with? Go visit Kevin Looney, see what happened to that poor guy's life. Fucked up forever at nineteen," Ellis spat the words at them before turning to go back to his desk.

Emily and Ryan walked out to the car. The afternoon sun was beginning its arc down to meet the ocean, where it would slowly disappear in a brilliant explosion of gold and pink, a classic California sunset.

"So, we've established from three legitimate sources now that Jaynes is basically the Browne family's stooge. He does what they want and gets paid a lot of money for it," Ryan said.

"Yeah, it looks that way," Emily agreed.

As she drove them back toward the FBI office in Westwood, Ellis' words kept repeating in her mind, like an old LP with the needle stuck: He *delivers whatever they ask him for.*

She wondered if that applied to Kaveri Browne.

Back at the FBI offices, Emily saw a note on her desk from Stephanie:

Former Browne family employee, Louise Niedermeier, now lives at El Sol Memory Care in Pasadena. Doesn't your dad live there?

Emily smiled, Stephanie could always be counted on to go the extra mile for an investigation. Emily's father, Michael Ray, had lived at El Sol for the past several years as his dementia progressed. She planned to speak to Louise Niedermeier since she had been with the Browne family for years when Kaveri disappeared. She and Ryan left for the day, with a plan to meet up the next morning after Emily's visit to Danica Hansen's biological family.

She was nervous, just the thought of seeing her mother made her feel sick to her stomach. Emily hadn't seen Amber Hansen since the day she drove away with her latest boyfriend, while Emily stood on the metal stairs of her aunt Janelle's trailer, watching their car disappear down the road. Earlier in the year, on the Josie Vance case, Emily had met with Janelle, accompanying Larissa Cinque, the same way she would today. That experience had been upsetting and infuriating, triggering her long-buried resentment and rage at the carelessness with which her family had treated her, setting her up to be the perfect victim of a predator like James Tibbs.

It had taken all of her self-control to maintain her composure, listening to Janelle weave together a false, self-serving narrative to absolve her of any responsibility. Emily could only imagine what Amber would have to say when questioned about her daughter's disappearance. She wished she had been able to beg off accompanying Larissa but she knew she needed to go and speak to them face to face, to figure out how and why they went along with Rawley Jaynes and his false claims. She knew her anxiety and PTSD would be flaring up as the night wore on and the next day's meeting drew closer. She did her box breathing exercises as she merged into the freeway traffic, hoping to calm her nervous system.

Half an hour later, as she inched her way through Downtown Los Angeles to La Cañada, she did her best to focus on the specifics of Kaveri Browne's case, to avoid drawing the inevitable comparisons to her own past. She looked out the window of her car, surrounded by a sea of red taillights, and felt panic overtaking her. Her breathing became shallow and she snapped the rubber band on her wrist several times but the feeling of being trapped crept up her limbs until she was fidgeting and restless, unable to sit still for a moment longer. Crossing several lanes of traffic, Emily pushed her way through, provoking shouts and rude gestures from other drivers, but she didn't care. She drove the side streets through Glassell Park, finally stopping outside a Mexican bakery where she got out of the car and leaned against the hood, dropping her head below her knees and taking deep breaths.

She closed her eyes but the image of her fifteen-year-old self filled her head. Lying awake in her bed, the sound of the ocean outside her window... knowing that at any moment someone would show up and reveal her as Danica Hansen.

Tossing and turning, under the summer coverlet, shutting her eyes tightly against the image of police cars arriving, of officers taking her by both arms and removing her from the life she had unjustly claimed as her own...

What if the police or the sheriffs came with no warning? What if the FBI investigated and sent her to prison for telling such a heinous lie? What if they found out... what if... what if...

She pushed the memory away, willing herself back to the present moment. She returned to her car and resumed driving. Even now as an adult she shuddered to think of the consequences if her truth had ever been discovered. She'd constructed such a full and rich life to tether her to the woman she had become, to keep her from being pulled back into the abyss she had escaped. Being on an investigation that required her to face all the possibilities of Kaveri Browne's abduction and return forced Emily to wade back into the deep, murky water of her own past. If Kaveri Browne were a fraud, Emily knew that there were desperate circumstances or desperate people behind it. The idea of exposing the young woman, when she herself had been living a lie for decades, made all of it even harder to bear.

And she could not make sense of Senator Harry Hubbard's interest in Kaveri Browne. There had to be something very valuable at stake for him to make the request of John Powers, and for the SAC to accept it. She hated being tasked with unraveling the elaborate webs of power that guided so many men in politics and in the high-level intelligence community. To call it a boys' club was an understatement in the extreme. Hubbard had a reputation in the Senate; he was a conniving old snake, and she had to discover his motives without being bitten first or sacrificed to his overarching greed and corruption.

As traffic broke and she picked up her pace, Emily pushed thoughts of the case from her mind, shifting her attention to her family plans for the evening. Dolores had picked the twins up from school and texted that they wanted Chinese takeout for dinner to make time to unpack the Christmas decorations. They would go to pick up the tree after dinner.

For seven years they had been going through the ritual of tree trimming with their daughters, getting the house ready for the holiday. She recalled the unpacking of ornaments, telling them the stories of how they found that blown-glass Santa Claus at a garage sale or how Antonio's mom made the papier mâché elves when he was a child. These were the small but important moments that formed the memories, the foundations of their family. The stories the girls would re-tell their own children someday. She felt tears coming on as she reflected on how this year, it was all different. She didn't know how she and Antonio would hide the tension and uncertainty between them while acting out a cherished family tradition, like characters in a holiday pantomime. It was going to be a long night.

As she reached the interchange to La Cañada, she impulsively took the exit toward El Sol Memory Care. She could pay her father a quick visit while looking into Louise Niedermeier, to see if she recalled anything of importance about Kaveri Browne.

She arrived at El Sol fifteen minutes later to find residents gathered in the community room, watching *Singing in the Rain* with Gene Kelly and Debbie Reynolds. The lights were dim, but she found her father, seated with two friends. His dementia was progressing, but he still recognized her easily when she tapped his arm.

"Emily! You're here, sit down. The show is almost over," he whispered, with a big smile.

They watched the remaining ten minutes of the movie and when the lights came on, the residents clapped as the kitchen staff circulated with decaf coffee and plates of cookies. Emily and Michael chatted about his day, the painting class he took and what he ate for lunch. Their conversations had become about such simple daily activities, but she was grateful for every moment they still had together.

She looked around the room at the women in their fluffy sweaters and Q-tip hairstyles, their fragile hands like dandelion puffs that might blow away in a breeze. She signaled one of the servers.

"Yes, Ms. Ray? Does your dad need anything?"

"No, thank you. Can I ask you something... which of these ladies is Louise Niedermeier?"

"Louise is the one in the wheelchair, by the window. She's very sweet, a little confused but quite lovely."

Louise wore matching white leisure wear and pink sneakers. She was chatting with her tablemates, smiling and laughing. When an attendant came to take her back to her room, Emily excused herself and met up with them in the hallway that led to the elevators.

"Excuse me. Ms. Niedermeier? My name is Emily Ray and my father lives here, on the second floor, Michael Ray."

Louise looked to Emily with a surprised smile. "Michael? He's on my floor, isn't he? The handsome man with the gray hair?"

The attendant nodded. "Yes, Louise. He's a few doors down from you."

"I wanted to know if you remember working for the Doucette-Browne family?" Emily asked.

Louise's expression shifted, her smile faded as she nodded her head slowly.

"Yes, at the big house. I worked at the big house with Gerte and Johan."

Emily crouched next to her wheelchair. "Do you remember Kaveri? Sierra's daughter?" she asked her gently.

Louise looked into Emily's eyes with a combination of fear and confusion.

"The baby? Miss Sierra's baby?"

"Yes, the little girl."

Louise shook her head, tears welling up in her eyes.

"The poor little thing. It was so awful. Her little body was so small and white..."

"Did something happen to Kaveri?" Emily asked quietly.

As Louise wept, her attendant gave Emily a warning glance.

"I'm sorry but you can't upset Louise this way. It's bedtime and she needs to stay calm before sleep," the attendant said, pushing the wheelchair forward.

As she moved away, Louise reached out and grabbed Emily's hand. "Did you see her? Before they put her in the orchard?"

"Time to say goodnight, Louise," the attendant said, moving down the hallway to the elevator. Emily watched them go. Louise's words pricked her curiosity, with a rising sense of foreboding.

Did you see her? Before they put her in the orchard?

TWELVE

Andy Ryan pulled into his apartment parking garage on Cloverdale Avenue in the Miracle Mile district, a bag of takeout from Andre's Italian Kitchen on the seat beside him. He'd been formulating a plan to dig into Rawley Jaynes and his incredibly good fortune in locating people who had been missing for decades when other law enforcement agencies had failed. At the office he'd visited Jaynes' new website that shared the same name as his book, *Home at Last*, to see how he solicited clients for his services.

Andy carried his dinner and a box of files into the elevator and rode to his third-floor apartment. He had only moved in six weeks earlier, when he and his partner, Erik, had split up. As he stepped in the front door, he felt a pang of discouragement at the paltry furnishings he had managed to acquire: a couch, a bookcase and an end table that his mother had given him. One lamp, a framed movie poster of *Cinema Paradiso* and a vintage liquor cart with one bottle of Jameson whiskey sitting on it, like a forlorn lighthouse. He'd been so busy with work, he simply hadn't had time to pick the pieces he wanted to live with every day, to figure out the window coverings. Erik had been better at all that, being in the arts, but Erik was gone.

After changing into sweats and a tee shirt, Ryan opened his

laptop at the kitchen counter and unpacked his takeout dinner from a local family run Italian restaurant that his elderly neighbor, Mr. Jacoves, had recommended. He didn't bother with plates or silverware; the heavy foil container and plastic forks were easier to deal with. He'd have time for domestic niceties at some point but this wasn't it. He had work to do.

He revisited Jaynes' website, filling out an online inquiry form. He used a separate email address that was only for investigative, undercover work and couldn't be traced to his personal or FBI profile. Years earlier, as a detective with the Redondo Beach Police Department, he had seen the need for a false online profile, given how much of life was now conducted on the internet.

He answered the online questionnaire, stating that his sister, Callie, had been missing for several years, abducted from Boulder, Colorado, and that he had saved up a significant amount of money to put toward finding her. He had no sister named Callie. He knew that if they sought Jaynes out as FBI agents, he wouldn't tell them anything about his operation since Ryan was almost certain it was a scam. But if he presented himself as Caleb Morgan, tormented younger brother of Callie Morgan, he might get some insight into how Jaynes positioned himself to potential clients.

He signed off as Caleb, adding that he was desperate and would appreciate a prompt response. He finished dinner and reviewed the file Powers had given them, still wondering why Senator Hubbard would be so interested in Kaveri Browne. He searched online for any scandals or improprieties that Hubbard had been involved in and found a pattern of allegations involving young men, most of whom had suddenly stopped talking about anything related to the senator, after going public with salacious claims of harassment or solicitation. It was assumed that their silence had been bought. One, twenty-two-year-old Joachim Cazu, had suspiciously fallen out of the tenth-story window of a hotel in Baltimore.

Ryan surmised that if Hubbard had been engaged in the types

of activities with young men that required silence, then he was easy to blackmail, ripe for extortion.

He was preparing for his evening shower when he got an email back from the Home at Last website and a woman named Zanie Lichtman, who presented herself as Rawley Jaynes' associate.

I can sense your desperation in your message, Mr. Morgan. I would be willing to meet with you as soon as tomorrow if that works for you, and we can discuss how to best help you find your sister, Callie.

Ryan high-fived himself in the bathroom mirror. He pulled out his undercover kit, kept in a plastic bin in his closet. It contained the things he had used several times as a detective, to change his appearance and avoid detection while conducting an investigation. He responded to Zanie Lichtman.

Thank you, Ms. Lichtman, I will make myself available in the morning. I have to be at work at noon so just let me know when and where and I will meet you. Thank you so very much!

He turned on the water in the shower and stepped in, considering what Caleb Morgan would look like and just how gullible he would be the next morning.

An hour later, Emily, Antonio, the twins and Dolores were walking through the Johnson Family Christmas tree lot, trying to decide which tree to bring home. The ground was covered with fresh sawdust and holiday music played from a large boom box at the cashier's shed. A handful of teenage boys were at the ready to attach the plastic water bowl and stand to the bottom of the tree while others were spraying white flocking on fat Douglas Firs. The fresh pine smell permeated the night air, calling forth long-cherished memories. This was always a special moment for them as a family, filled with the delectable anticipation of the coming holidays: the gingerbread cookie making, the school parties, the Christmas carol sing-alongs at the local park. A few weeks in the busy year when they could celebrate the love and connection of family life. This year, however, it didn't feel the same.

Antonio walked ahead of Emily and Dolores, the twins gripping his hands and directing him toward this perfect tree or that one. Emily felt as if she were watching herself through a lens, outside of her body. She looked at Antonio's back, his black hair curling at the neckline of the Patagonia fleece pullover she gave him the previous year. And all she could think of was he and Anjelica Romero together, being intimate while she was busy at work with no idea what was going on.

As if she could read Emily's mind, Dolores took her arm and said, "It will be a strange Christmas this year."

"If we make it fun for the girls, they won't notice anything," Emily said.

"They notice a lot, Emilia. More than you think. They're smart, they know that something is going on. But you're right, not to just make everything okay the way Toño wants. What he did was unforgivable. I don't know how he could be so stupid. And reckless."

"Me, either," she agreed sadly.

"I know people say you're not supposed to take sides, but I do. I'm on your side," Dolores said, squeezing Emily's hand in support.

Emily watched her husband inspecting a Noble Fir like a civil engineer inspecting a damaged bridge. She smiled, in spite of herself. He was such a nerdy goofball sometimes.

"Thanks, Dolores. I'm just taking one day at a time."

A worker dressed up as one of Santa's elves appeared in a lopsided hat and plastic elfin ears to take photos with the children at the tree lot. Dolores corralled the girls into the line while Emily watched Antonio measuring the tree's width and height. Her phone rang; it was Lydia, her therapist.

"Emily, I just wanted to check in before our Zoom appointment on Friday. Everything going okay? The holiday season can be tough, even at the best of times," Lydia said.

"Yeah. We're out picking up the Christmas tree. We're decorating tonight. What fun," Emily said sarcastically.

"Ugh, sorry. That's a hard one. Remember, most of it is a bunch of fabricated, sentimental manipulation. Everyone feels like their family is crazy and messed up at this time of year. Except the ones who really are."

Emily laughed weakly. "I'll remember that."

"Do you feel any closer to a decision about moving forward? Or not?"

"No, not really. I keep hoping I'm going to wake up one morning and feel like I've finally crossed that hurdle and I'm ready to move forward and fix everything. But I just don't feel that way. I'm so... angry and the betrayal just sits right there, on my chest. Like a rock," Emily said, her conflict roiling inside her.

"Then you don't know yet. You may never feel that way, Em. It may not be fixable and if that's the case, you'll know when it's time to let it all go. I know it's hard to just sit with it. How's work? Have you decided which division to move to?" Lydia asked.

"I'm on an investigation into Kaveri Miller Browne who just returned after being kidnapped eighteen years ago."

"Jesus! Life is throwing everything at you right now! That hits a little close to home, doesn't it?"

"Yeah, but I think that's why the SAC chose me," Emily whispered into the phone.

"Stay in touch, okay? You're dealing with a lot. See you Friday."

"Will do. Thanks, Lydia."

Emily hung up as her daughters ran to her, grabbing her hands to show her the two finalists in the tree contest. One was a fat, bushy Noble Fir and one was an elegant blue Spruce.

"I like the one with the separate branches so we can see the ornaments better," Juli's eyes were shining with glee.

"But the other one is fat and there's more room for all the decorations!" Liza insisted excitedly.

"Let's spin Mommy around and see which one she chooses!" Juli said, grabbing Emily and spinning her in a circle.

"Keep your eyes closed!" Liza shouted, joining in. "Whichever one you point to is the one we're taking home!"

"Okay, I'm not peeking... and the one I choose is you!"

Emily opened her eyes and saw that she was pointing directly at Antonio, who gave her a hopeful smile.

"Daddy doesn't count! The tree closest to him is the spruce! That's the one!" Juli said, grabbing Antonio's hand and running off to find someone to help load up the tree.

Emily watched them go, wishing life's decisions were as simple as spinning in a circle in a child's game. An overwhelming sense of sadness came over her; the loss of everything that had been and would never be the same again.

Danica Hansen pulled up to her family's home in Baker later than she had expected. The traffic from L.A. to Vegas was heavy. Baker was a drive-through town, a stopover for people who needed fast food, gas or coffee. Many of the businesses were closed and boarded up, some buildings were just empty hulls of metal wiring and cinderblocks, covered with graffiti. Of the roughly four hundred residents, Roy and Hilda Sanders had one of the neat, tidy bungalows with a proper fence and Astroturf grass that stayed green all year long. They were surrounded by the vast Mojave Desert, dusty, dry and unforgiving.

Danica rolled down the window of her car and took a deep breath. She loved the smell of the desert at night, and she took comfort in the stark desolation. She heard a pack of coyotes yipping from somewhere close by, chasing down an unfortunate prey. Oddly, she felt safe out here, with Roy and Hilda and their small routine that never changed much.

A grocery trip once a week to the Stater Brothers' supermarket in Barstow, where they would stock up on items not found at the local Baker Market. In Barstow they'd visit a few other chain stores and eat at a small, local Mexican restaurant called La Posada. Or they'd stop at Eddie World in Yermo and get hand-churned ice cream.

Back at home, they'd check the generators once a month and make sure they were stocked up with gas. When winter approached, they'd gather kindling and old wood from the surrounding desert to make sure they had enough to light the fireplace on cold, desert nights. By October the night air was chilly and by December, the moment the sun went down the temperature dropped dramatically. The rhythm of her life was so predictable, it wrapped her in a safe cocoon of a steady routine that offered few surprises. She didn't like surprises.

Danica sat in the quiet of the night; she could see the blue light of the television on in the living room. She knew that when she went in, she would find her mother, Hilda, asleep on the couch, waiting for her to return, like she always did. She'd given up asking her parents for more details on how she came to live with them and her life with Coralee Buell. They both got quiet or upset when she pushed for an explanation that made sense to this whole Danica Hansen business. So, she had stopped. There was no need to upset her dad when he was already battling cancer.

She hoped Zanie had been wrong and there would be no more appearances or magazine interviews about her miraculous discovery. Zanie and Mr. Jaynes had told her not to speak to any reporters or others who came digging around for information, now that her story was out. She was to refer them to Zanie. She hoped no one showed up and that no one had any further interest in her. She wanted to remain Shirelle Sanders. She didn't like being Danica Hansen. Not at all.

THIRTEEN

Emily slept fitfully. Keeping up a front for the girls, smiling and not showing any sign of the sadness, confusion, hurt and anger she felt was exhausting. Dolores had put on Christmas music and made traditional champurrado and the rich, chocolatey scent of it brought tears to her eyes, remembering the first time Antonio had taken her downtown to pick a Christmas tree at the Union Station train tracks, and they'd had steaming champurrado in Styrofoam cups. Juli and Liza thought she was getting sentimental about the ornaments, but she could see that Antonio knew better. The pain on his face was clear, but she could not meet his eyes.

The king-sized bed in the main bedroom felt too large and she kept moving from one side to the other. But it wasn't just the weight of Christmas that kept her on edge. It was the knowledge that in a few hours, she'd be sitting across from her real mother and aunt, accompanying Larissa Cinque on her interview about Rawley Jaynes. She wondered what the fake Danica Hansen was doing right now. Was she out at a trendy restaurant with Jaynes, setting up magazine interviews and investigating how to cash in on her new notoriety? She fully expected to see Danica Hansen on the cover of *People* or a Lifetime movie about her.

Emily lay in bed, staring at the ceiling, considering the possibilities. Surely, the woman pretending to be Danica Hansen had to know she was a fraud? Or maybe, she was pliable and easy to mislead, and it was all the work of Rawley Jaynes. But why take such a huge risk of being found out? What incentive could she possibly have for going along with such a deception?

Emily's mind was stuck in a cycle that she had to break. She grabbed the rubber band she had removed from her wrist to sleep and slipped it over her wrist. She snapped it hard, several times, hoping the sting would break her out of an obsessive thought spiral. It didn't work. She was stuck in a tunnel, unable to stop asking the same questions again and again, as if her mind would suddenly have a miraculous breakthrough.

What did Danica Hansen stand to gain from taking on a fake identity? And what did Rawley Jaynes gain from promoting her as such? In Jaynes' case, it was easy. He was launching a book and starting a new business venture. He needed more than the one high-profile success story he had with Kaveri Browne. He needed someone else to bolster his claims of being able to do what the police detectives and the FBI couldn't. By all accounts he was a braggart and a bullshitter, but he had to have a system and a specific profile he looked for when searching out victims. She just had to figure out what angle he was working. Perhaps Amber Hansen, and her sister Janelle, would give up some clues. She finally drifted to sleep in the early hours of the morning.

By seven a.m, she was on her way to the South Bay, to meet Larissa at a local Chili's restaurant where she would interview Amber and Janelle. She wanted to get there early, even if it just meant sitting in her car, waiting. It was Antonio's day to take the girls to school and Dolores was doing the pick-up. She left Juli and Liza notes with funny drawings sticking out of the cereal box so they would be amused. She needed time to prepare for the day ahead.

. . .

Andy Ryan sat at a back table at Dupars in the Farmer's Market across from Zanie Lichtman. He had put washout highlights into his light brown hair and styled it with gel to give the top a tousled look. He'd trimmed up the sides, so he'd look like a million other guys sporting a classic quiff along with designer stubble. To finish the look he wore a pair of clear glasses, a silk, block-pattern button-down shirt and tight black skinny jeans. Zanie believed him to be a graphic designer from Colorado, living in L.A.

She had a stack of paperwork with her, taking notes as she asked him about his sister's disappearance.

"So, Callie went out with friends and the last time she was seen was in a parking lot in downtown Boulder?" Zanie asked, her eyes filled with compassion.

"Yeah. She was visiting friends who went to school there and they'd gone out for drinks. A guy at the bar was talking with her a lot, kind of bothering her. And then when they all left, she walked to her car alone and... that was it," Ryan said, his voice cracking.

"And you filed a missing persons case with the Boulder Police?"

"They didn't do anything. They acted like she was a wild college kid who probably went off with her boyfriend. But she didn't even have a boyfriend! I hired a PI but he didn't do much and when I saw Mr. Jaynes on that TV show, I thought maybe he could help."

"And you have photos of Callie from that time?"

"I have a bunch. I can email them to you, if that works."

"That will be fine. Mr. Jaynes is out meeting with other clients at the moment, but this is how we work. We require a ten-thou-sand-dollar retainer up front and with that we begin the investiga-tion. We look into all of Callie's friends and acquaintances at that time, and we review the police reports. We speak to any and all possible witnesses and dig into the background of anyone she had contact with. We try to piece together a trajectory for where she went, where she was seen, who she interacted with, any banking or cell phone records. Putting a fresh set of eyes on this information is imperative because no matter what they say, the police aren't doing anything," Zanie explained.

"But how do you zero in on a possible person? Like, how did you guys know that Kaveri Browne was who she was?"

Zanic looked surprised at the question then recovered. "Well, it would be a bit different with your sister. In Kaveri's case, we looked at birth records and other information that might be related since she was so young when she disappeared. Same with Danica. Your sister always lived with you and your parents?"

Ryan nodded, his interest piqued by the mention of birth certificates and other identification documents.

Zanie continued. "Are your parents alive? Do they want to find Callie as well or are they ready to close that painful chapter? Some families are, you know."

Ryan said, "No, our parents are dead. It's just me."

Zanie pursed her lips and slid several pieces of paper across the table to him. "This is the contract. We can't make any guarantees, given how difficult this type of work is. But this truly is the best chance you have of finding out what happened to your sister."

Ryan looked over the contract and asked, "Why do you need my permission to run my credit?"

"That's just standard procedure at our company. It's a formality, really," Zanie said with a big smile. Ryan pretended to be confused, perusing the documents.

"Can I take these home and think about it? It's such a big step and the retainer is pretty pricey," he said.

"Of course, Caleb. Take all the time you need. Mr. Jaynes' schedule is filling up, but I know he'd love to get some answers for you."

"Thank you, Ms. Lichtman. You'll hear from me within the next few days," Ryan said, shaking her hand politely before he left.

Zanie watched him go, confident they would hear back from him soon. She believed wholeheartedly that he had been struggling with Callie's disappearance for a long time. The fact that his sister was already an adult when she went missing made things more complicated. It was much easier when the subject disappeared as a child; she and Rawley would have a lot more wiggle room to work with. And it was unfortunate the parents were gone as well.

Sometimes it helped to have family members who were so broken and tired of hoping, that they were willing to make the investigation into a win-win for everyone. Callie Morgan would be more of a challenge but then again, she and Rawley made no promises. Ten thousand dollars could be used up quickly while delving into the history of a subject. And ten thousand dollars was ten thousand dollars.

Emily had arrived early at the Chili's restaurant parking lot; she wanted to be able to see her mother arrive, before sitting across a table from her. She watched from her car as Larissa parked and within a few minutes Amber and Janelle pulled up in a spanking new Toyota Highlander. Amber looked washed-out and much older than Emily imagined she would be. But her recollections were stuck in a kind of emotional time warp, twenty-three years earlier. Amber barely resembled the woman Emily could still see so clearly in her mind, walking away with a casual wave to a ten-year-old girl, who stood stiff with anxiety and fear at being abandoned, again.

Amber and Janelle seemed excited, almost giddy, as they entered the restaurant. Emily drew in a deep breath, to prepare herself. She felt the bitter disbelief that no matter how much she had tried to put the specter of Danica Hansen to rest, she was about to dredge up the memories of that forgotten girl, with the very people who should have protected her but failed.

There would never be any escape from that fear hanging over her. The day she chose to become Emily Ray, to surrender her identity as an inconsequential, invisible teenager named Danica Hansen, she had spent a lifetime looking over her shoulder, of never being able to exhale and live in peace. Perhaps that was the price to be paid for deception. She took a deep breath and went inside.

She saw Larissa seated at a table across from Janelle and Amber. The restaurant was crowded with people eating breakfast, the air smelled of hot pancakes and syrup, and freshly brewed coffee. Emily walked toward them, feeling as if she were moving in slow motion, being inexorably pulled toward where the three women sat. She arrived at the table, her heart pounding as she looked directly into her mother's eyes and saw not even a glimmer of recognition.

"I'm Emily Ray, nice to meet you, Mrs. Hansen," she said, extending her hand.

Amber took her hand, warmly. "Amber Hansen." Her voice was raspy, her teeth brittle and yellow from years of smoking.

"I met you earlier this year, right? When you were working on that kidnapping of the little girl from PV, right?" Janelle asked, eyeing Emily suspiciously.

"Yes. Josie Vance," Emily replied.

"Special Agent Ray is giving me her input on the amazing discovery of Kaveri Miller Browne and Danica. She's worked with the FBI for years in kidnapping cases and since she met Janelle last year for my story on Danica, I thought it would be good for her to be here," Larissa explained to Amber.

Amber shifted uneasily. "Is the FBI looking into Danica?"

"No, not at all. Larissa just wanted my input on the interview today," Emily assured her.

"Well, we didn't know what happened to her, you know? She just disappeared, didn't come home one day. And of course, we reported her missing right away," Janelle explained.

"I'm sorry, in my research earlier this year, the police confirmed that no report was filed for Danica until she had been missing for several weeks," Larissa said.

Amber shot a look at Janelle. "I was out of the state, and my sister was taking care of Dani. I didn't even know she was missing for some time."

"So, how did Mr. Jaynes contact you?" Larissa asked.

Janelle spoke up, "He called one day and asked about Dani. Said he might have found her, all grown up and living with a different family. You could'a knocked me over with a feather!"

"Didn't it seem strange? That she was taken by a random woman named Coralee Buell? Most disappearances of children don't work that way," Emily said.

"Well, sure. But like Mr. Jaynes said, sometimes it's not a bad guy, it's just someone who... wants a kid," Amber said, nervously.

"That has not been my experience, with the FBI CARD team. It's usually a crime committed by a family member or acquaintance. Or a predator, of course. I don't think I've ever had a case involving a nice person who just wanted a kid, as you say," Emily said, dryly, her gaze fixed on Amber's pale blue eyes. She could tell she was making her mother uncomfortable but she didn't care. Amber finally looked away and fiddled with the strap of her purse.

"I assume you were shocked to hear that. Danica had been missing for so long, what did you think happened to her?" Larissa asked.

"I thought she'd just run off. My sister couldn't handle her, that's why she left her with me," Janelle said, self-importantly.

"That's not true!" Amber retorted. "I didn't know what had happened. I hoped it wasn't a bad person who took her."

Emily fought the urge to laugh sarcastically at their phony posturing, rewriting the truth of what had really happened. She looked away, unable to bear the sight of Amber and Janelle, thinking back to the five years of trauma and misery she'd spent with James Tibbs while the two women across the table never gave her a second thought. She clenched her palms into a fist to control her rage.

"How did Danica react when she met you again?" Larissa asked.

"She was surprised, for sure. Not sure what to make of us!" Janelle snorted. "She was all shy, kind of nervous. But we got on."

"What reasons did Mr. Jaynes have for thinking he had found the right woman, after all these years?" Emily asked, trying to keep her voice even. She could feel the sweat pooling in her neck and the smell of bacon in the air was turning her stomach.

"He said that... he'd found a woman who matched Dani's appearance, and she didn't have the proper birth certificate or something; it caught his eye. Something seemed off and then he looked deeper into her situation," Janelle explained.

Emily noticed Amber staring intently at her. She smiled, uncomfortably.

"Is something wrong, Mrs. Hansen?" Emily asked.

Amber shook her head slowly. "No, I just noticed that little mole under your bottom lip. Danica had one in the same place."

Emily felt her heart rate slow. Her vision blurred for a moment. The part of her that desperately wanted her mother to recognize her collided with the part that was trembling with dread at the prospect of it. It took several seconds for her to find her voice and recover.

"Oh, that mole came up when I was in college," Emily shrugged. "I guess they are fairly common."

Amber cocked her head and nodded.

"So, at what point did you feel ready to run a DNA test?" Larissa cut in.

"Soon as Rawley said what was in it. We wanted to know right away!" Janelle replied with a laugh, and Amber shot her a cautionary look.

"What do you mean, 'what was in it'?" Emily asked more sharply than she'd intended.

"She didn't mean nothing. Just that we might finally know what really happened to Dani, that's all," Amber said quickly.

Emily nodded; she was one step closer to discovering exactly what was behind Rawley Jaynes and his miraculous discoveries.

As the interview wrapped up, they left the restaurant together.

Emily said her goodbyes and headed toward her car. She took in a big gulp of fresh air to steady the nausea that lingered. But before she could take another deep breath, Amber called after her. Emily turned back to her, instinctively placing her hands in a sideways T-shape to shield them from the bright sunlight.

"Yes, Mrs. Hansen?"

"I just wanted to thank you for caring about Dani and wanting to find out more about her now that she's back. It's funny..." Amber said.

"What is?" Emily asked.

"The way you put your hands up to block the sun, like a crooked T. Dani used to do it the very same way!"

Emily nodded and got into her car, her fingers shaking as she turned the key in the ignition. She hadn't expected Amber to remember anything about her as a child. She checked her rearview mirror as she pulled away and saw her mother watching her car disappear down the busy boulevard.

FOURTEEN

An hour later, Emily and Ryan were driving from the FBI offices to Holmby Hills to attempt a face-to-face meeting with Mackenzie Browne.

"I can't believe that you came up with this guy, Caleb Morgan. I wish I had seen you in those skinny jeans!" Emily said, as he recounted his meeting with Zanie.

"That's never happening. It's helpful to have a persona like that already set up. Caleb has dating profiles, I even made a few websites that look like real companies that he worked at. I have a separate burner phone for those fake companies. It's kind of cool."

"If you were a weirdo, you could use those dating profiles to meet real people," Emily suggested.

Ryan laughed. "Right. That's a pretty big weirdo! What I thought was interesting is that Zanie Lichtman didn't give me any details about their business model, beyond the basic ones that anyone could figure out. I can't imagine why they need to run credit checks on clients," he said.

"Maybe it's like the FBI, they want to see if someone is in financial trouble and susceptible to blackmail or bribery," Emily said. "They make us submit to credit checks."

"Sure, but we work for the Federal Government, we're not some skanky, bottom-feeder private investigator."

"There's most likely a money angle. I'm sure Jaynes miraculously finding these people is a scam. I just haven't figured out how to connect all the pieces together yet," Emily said.

"And speaking of blackmail, Senator Harry Hubbard looks like a prime candidate given all the rumors and the accusers who have suddenly shut up," Ryan said.

"Doesn't it feel like everyone involved in this is somehow shady?" Emily asked.

"Maybe that's why it's an off-the-books favor rather than a real investigation," Ryan mused.

Emily turned off Sunset onto Beverly Glen Boulevard and into the Holmby Hills area. At the Doucette-Browne compound, a group of photographers were already lying in wait, as close as was legally allowed, in the hopes of getting a photo of the young heiress. Emily pulled up to a security kiosk with an electric gate, flashing her FBI badge at the guard.

"Hello, I'm Special Agent Emily Ray with the FBI. This is Special Agent Andy Ryan. We're hoping to speak to Mackenzie Miller Browne," she said.

The guard eyed her suspiciously. "Do you have an appointment?"

"No, we don't. Could you check to see if she's available?" Emily asked, with a smile.

The guard remained wary and said, "Everyone needs to have an appointment, but I guess I can check."

Emily could see that he was afraid of making a mistake of any kind, but the weight of the FBI seemed to intimidate him, as she had hoped. He spoke to someone on a phone and then opened the gate.

"Follow the road until the quadrangle. You'll see a cluster of homes. Ms. Mackenzie's is the white plantation-style house. Please sign in, and I also have to take a photo of your identification," he said, handing Emily a clipboard with a thick sign-in sheet before walking around the car, noting the license plate, then snapping photos of their FBI badges and ID cards.

"Thank you very much," Emily said, as they pulled into the compound.

"I can't believe she let us in, just showing up unannounced," Ryan said.

"Maybe she has no reason to be nervous about us," Emily speculated. "This could just be a whole lot of nothing driven by Harry Hubbard."

"The whole thing is weird," Ryan mumbled.

As they drove down the winding road, they passed the lush gardens; a topiary of animals covered one large area, and a pair of peacocks stood among them, the male spreading his impressive feathers and strutting in front of the female in a mating dance.

"This place is like a park!" Ryan marveled. "I've never seen peacocks running loose before."

"Visit Arcadia. They're all over the place, pooping on lawns. They chase you sometimes, and they're mean."

"No, thanks," Ryan said, with a laugh.

They came around a corner and found the quadrangle of residences. The large main house could only be classified as a mansion, set on a hill, overlooking the others past a terraced rise of flowering shrubs and tall Italian Cypress trees. As they parked outside Mackenzie Browne's house, she came out to greet them, confident and relaxed in a beige unstructured suit, her caramel-colored hair pulled back in a casual ponytail.

"I'm Mackenzie Miller Browne. To what do I owe the pleasure of a visit from the FBI?" she asked, warmly.

"Thank you for seeing us without any notice," Emily said. "This is my colleague, Special Agent Andy Ryan."

"Please, come in. Can I offer you some coffee or tea?" Mackenzie asked, her tone polished and poised, a perfect hostess. Emily took in the lush, expensive furnishings and the cavernous rooms that extended beyond the living room and adjacent sunroom.

"No, thank you," Emily said. "This is a beautiful house."

"Thank you. There are a handful of them, for family members who want to stay close. It makes security easier, and it can be consolidated. How can I help you?"

"We saw your appearance on *The World Today* and we just have a few questions regarding your granddaughter, Kaveri."

Mackenzie smiled but Emily could see the coolness in her eyes. "Kaveri? What questions?"

"I'm the former head of the FBI Child Abduction Rapid Deployment team and very familiar with the procedure for finding children who have been kidnapped. Mr. Jaynes' success rate with two victims after all these years is truly exceptional," Emily explained, watching Mackenzie's reaction closely, but she remained unflappable and relaxed.

"Yes, and?" Mackenzie asked.

"I wanted to know if you could give us some backstory on Kaveri's disappearance and how she was found," Emily asked.

"And why would I do that?" Mackenzie replied, with a tight, polite smile. "She's been found; her DNA has been confirmed. We have nothing to hide, nor do we owe anyone or any agency an explanation of her case, which is finally closed after all these years."

Emily nodded, she knew she was on precarious ground with her inquiry and Mackenzie Browne was not naïve. She made a split-second decision to tell the truth.

"I know. We received a request to verify her identity, and we don't have a lot of information as to the reasons someone is asking for that."

"So, you're saying that anyone can call the FBI and request you to verify a citizen's identity, and they send you two out like bloodhounds?" she asked, still smiling amiably but her voice betrayed a slight edge of impatience. Or something else.

"No, not just any random person," Emily said, aware that what she left unsaid opened a sink hole of speculation.

"Well, that's an unpleasant job, showing up at someone's home and asking about the veracity of their granddaughter's identity. I didn't know we were at the point where the government can do that. This isn't Germany in 1940."

"It's a strange request and you have no obligation to speak to us. This was a case that the bureau worked, and we're always interested when there is a positive outcome, even if it is years later," Emily lied.

Mackenzie's eyes narrowed. "Or do you think someone doubts Kaveri? Who do you imagine that would be? Her mother, Sierra? My father, who is overjoyed to have his only surviving great-grandchild back?"

At that moment, Sierra entered from the dining room, holding a bag of lemons.

"I'm sorry, I didn't realize you had company," she said, apologizing.

"This isn't a social visit, dear. Let me introduce my daughter, Sierra Miller Browne," Mackenzie said tersely. "How long have you been here, Sierra? I didn't see you come in."

"You didn't? I saw you and waved, and I called out when I came in to get these lemons. My trees just aren't bearing fruit this year and my mother's are prolific lemon producers," Sierra said, with a nervous laugh.

Emily noted the strained quality of their interaction and Mackenzie's annoyance at her daughter's sudden appearance. She sensed that Sierra had overheard the conversation about Kaveri.

"Nice to meet you, Sierra. I'm sure you can answer this: what type of name is Kaveri? It's so lovely but I've never heard it before," Emily asked.

"Kaveri is a river in south India. It means 'one who brings abundance where she flows,'" Sierra said.

Mackenzie scoffed. "That was during the eastern religions phase of Sierra's life. Everything was about India and meditation and wearing madras-print clothing. And beads, of course."

Sierra ignored her and asked, "Do you have any other questions about Kaveri?"

Before Emily or Ryan could answer, Mackenzie stood and guided Sierra to the door.

"They're very busy and so are you, my dear. This doesn't concern you at all. Aren't you supposed to be working on the redesign of the Japanese gardens?"

"It was nice to meet you," Sierra said, pulling against her mother's grip on her arm.

Once she was gone, Mackenzie turned back to Emily and Ryan, taking her seat again. "Sierra can be easily agitated and flighty. It's best for her to keep to a firm schedule and limit any emotional turbulence that can throw her off course. Where were we?"

"I know this inquiry about Kaveri is awkward and uncomfortable," Emily began, but Mackenzie cut her off.

"Did it come from Harry Hubbard?" she asked.

"I'm not at liberty to say," Emily replied, hiding her surprise.

Mackenzie shook her head and sighed, as if a pesky ant had somehow managed to climb onto the hem of her pants.

"Which is a politic way of saying 'yes' without saying 'yes.' I can tell you this, Special Agent Ray, Senator Hubbard has... issues. He is a longtime associate of my father's, and he has an unhealthy fascination with the workings of our family. If he made this outrageous request, all I can advise is that you dismiss it as the obsession of a grasping political hack who sees his own future fading with each passing season. You are government employees trying to do what is asked of you. But as a family, we have no further comment on Kaveri Miller Browne and her miraculous return to us," Mackenzie said, standing to signal that the meeting was over.

Emily nodded and stood to leave with Ryan who followed suit. His face was red with embarrassment and Emily felt the sting of Mackenzie's words as they excused themselves.

As they walked to the car, Ryan said, "God! I feel like an idiot! She said 'government employees' like we're cockroaches!"

Emily slowed her pace, scanning the quadrangle. "She's a wealthy, powerful woman who is accustomed to shutting down questions she doesn't want to answer. And she's right, she doesn't owe anyone an explanation. But now I want to see what this visit shakes out."

"She and her daughter clearly have a tough relationship. She's so demeaning to Sierra, I can only imagine what she's like to Kaveri," Ryan said.

Emily saw Sierra on the porch of her house, kitty corner to Mackenzie's. A new Honda CRV sat in the driveway. Emily jotted the license plate number into her phone.

"Can't be easy living right across the quad from her. It's got to be like having a handler, watching everything you do," she said.

"I got the sense that Mackenzie wants it that way," Ryan said.

"If you had this much money, would you buy a new Honda?" Emily asked, getting into her car.

"No, I'd buy a fully loaded Audi or a Rivian."

"Right. Or a Benz or a Jaguar. A status car," Emily agreed. "Unless you want to differentiate yourself from what is expected of you. Or break free of it."

Emily backed the car out and headed toward the security kiosk. In her rearview mirror, she saw Mackenzie had come out and stood watching them from her front walkway.

"Mackenzie Browne wants to make sure we're gone," Ryan added, checking her out in the side mirror.

"We have to find a way to get to Sierra or Kaveri, on their own without big mama Mackenzie standing guard. I want to hear what they have to say about this whole thing," Emily said, waving to the security guard who stared them down as they drove past.

"And we have to talk to Danica Hansen as soon as possible," Ryan said.

Emily nodded in agreement, but she felt her courage flag. She was determined to avoid a face to face with the newly found Danica Hansen, turning over every stone she could to avoid it. If they focused on Kaveri, they might get the answers they needed.

As Emily's car pulled off the compound and the electric gate closed behind her, Mackenzie stood watch, to be certain the car disappeared down the tree-lined street. She kicked at a dried magnolia seed pod that had fallen on her walkway with the tip of her Louboutin black leather pump. She hadn't believed that Harry Hubbard would go so far as to call in favors from the FBI but now that he had thrown down the gauntlet, she would retaliate. She knew what he wanted.

She called an international number that would be routed through three different countries until it arrived in an underground office in Tel Aviv. No one ever answered this line; it was for messages only and a person using the pseudonym Gideon would call back. She left a message and hung up. Her hands were shaking with rage she could not contain.

She left her house and stormed up the marble stairs to the big house, without letting Sozi or Gerte know she was coming to see her father. Once inside she hurried to his room on the second story and pushed the door open. Sozi was playing a game on her phone while Jinx dozed.

"You can leave, Sozi. I must speak to my father privately," Mackenzie said brusquely.

"Are you sure I shouldn't stay to help you with him, Miss Mackenzie?"

"I said *leave*. Now!" Mackenzie shouted at her and Sozi scurried out, closing the door behind her.

Mackenzie approached her father, who seemed completely unaware of her presence.

"Did you do it, Jinx? Did you get that weasel Hubbard to do your dirty work for you?" she whispered fiercely in his ear. "Is this another one of your sick, twisted games?"

The old man did not respond, and she grabbed his frail wrist tightly. It felt as if it would snap beneath her grip.

"I know you can hear me, no matter how feeble you pretend you are. If you put those FBI agents onto Kaveri or if your lapdog Hubbard did it on his own, call it off now. Or I will make the short remainder of your miserable existence a living hell!" she hissed.

His eyelids fluttered briefly then closed again. She looked at him in disgust and left.

As she crossed the quadrangle back to her own house, she pulled her phone out to dial Rawley Jaynes. It went to voicemail.

"I just had two FBI agents at my door asking about Kaveri. Call me. Immediately!"

FIFTEEN

Rawley Jaynes threw his cell phone against the wall of the kitchen, the screen shattering and the body denting as it bounced onto the marble countertop. He had just listened to Mackenzie's message, and his mind was like a whirlpool, spinning wildly and sucking him down into its vortex. How the hell had an FBI agent gotten involved in Kaveri's case? Who could've tipped them off or raised any suspicion?

He paced, picking up the pieces of his broken phone, immediately regretting the destruction. He needed to talk to Zanie, she would dig into this disaster and put a stop to it. He heard her car pull up in the circular driveway. He hurried outside to meet her as she got out of the car carrying several shopping bags.

"We've got trouble. Mackenzie just called and left a voice message to say that two FBI agents showed up at her place, asking about Kaveri!"

The color drained from Zanie's face for a moment, then she recovered. "Okay, let's deal with one thing at a time. They came by today? Which means they saw *The World Today* segment yesterday."

"I'm sure that's it. I haven't called her back yet, I wanted to talk to you first," he said, running his hands through his hair, nervously.

"Good boy, Rawley. Let's call her right now and get more details," Zanie said, setting her packages down and leading him to the big leather sofa. "I have some good news. I think we got a new client today."

"Great. I threw my phone against the wall and broke it," he admitted, like a guilty child.

Zanie fixed him with an exasperated look. "Aren't we a little too old for that?" she asked, as she dialed Mackenzie's number and put the call on speaker.

"Hi, Zanie. I assume Rawley told you the news?" Mackenzie said, her voice tight with tension.

"Yes, he did. I need to know the names of both agents so I can look into their backgrounds and how the connection was made," Zanie said, working hard to appear calm when she was having a silent meltdown.

"Special Agent Emily Ray and Andy Ryan. She seems to be the lead and said they worked child abductions for the FBI and had some questions about Kaveri's reappearance," Mackenzie said. "You have to shut this down. We can't have Kaveri's return to a normal life disrupted by this kind of spurious investigation. It had no merit; it would only cause her distress as well as a world of problems for us!"

"You think? I'm not worried about Kaveri's return to normal life, Mackenzie! We have bigger things to deal with if they stay on this!" Rawley said.

"I'll look into this and figure out where it came from," Zanie said, her fingers working furiously on her laptop keyboard. "The FBI investigated Kaveri's disappearance years ago and came up with nothing. Could it be that they're just looking into it because it was their case and was never closed?"

"Maybe. But I asked about someone my father knows, and from Agent Ray's response, I think it might have come from him," Mackenzie said.

"Who is it?" Zanie asked.

"Senator Harry Hubbard."

Rawley's eyes got as big as dinner plates, and he let out a sound that was something between a whistle and a groan.

"A fucking Senator? Why would he care about Kaveri?" he demanded.

"He's off his rocker, really. My dad has given him a lot of money over the years and I think he's just obsessed with what goes on in our family now," Mackenzie said.

"But why would Kaveri's identity have anything to do with that?" Zanie asked, plainly.

Mackenzie replied, "I have no idea. Please find out what you can, about the FBI agents and how to shut them down. I don't care how it's handled. I'll speak to everyone here who's involved in any of the family businesses or charities. We need everyone to keep silent and give them nothing."

"I'll put one of our people on it. We'll keep an eye on both agents, so we know what they're up to."

"Thank you, that would be very helpful," Mackenzie said, hanging up.

Rawley was on the verge of hyperventilating on the sofa, his broad face was shiny with flop-sweat. Zanie knew he wasn't going to be much help in dealing with the FBI situation. She also knew that Mackenzie Browne hadn't told them the whole story.

"So, what do we do next?" Rawley asked.

"We just keep moving forward. We have a game plan, and one little glitch isn't going to change that."

Rawley laughed hoarsely. "I think the FBI is more than a little glitch!"

"We have a new client, Caleb Morgan. He's trying to find his sister who disappeared a few years ago."

"An adult? That's going to be harder," he said. "But you told him about the retainer, right?"

"Yes. He'll be getting back to us in a day or so. This might be one where we don't get the happy ending, but we get paid. So, it's a happy ending for us."

Rawley stood up and paced anxiously. "It's hard to think of anything else besides the fucking FBI!"

"I'm putting Norayr on them as a tail. To see where they go, where they live. We'll keep close tabs on them. You need to calm down, go take a Xanax and lie down for a while. I'll handle everything," Zanie said.

Rawley nodded and went into the bedroom, taking a plastic bottle of Xanax out of a dresser drawer and popping one into his mouth. He wished he had something stronger, like the old days of a big, fat Oxycontin prescription every month. He lay down on the bed and thought of their go-to handyman, Norayr Apelian, a member of the Armenian Power 13 gang in Glendale. He'd done lots of odd jobs for Rawley over the years. He could deal with the FBI agents if it became necessary. Rawley closed his eyes and willed himself to fall asleep and forget about all of it. For now.

Kaveri climbed out of the pool and grabbed the big plush towel to dry off. The water was kept a perfect eighty-three degrees, even in the winter. The weather was mild and warm, even just a few weeks before Christmas. She laid down on a chaise longue and squinted up at the sky. In the distance on the compound, she heard one of the gardeners blowing leaves. She instinctively grabbed her phone to text Trina but thought better of it. Despite their lifelong friendship, Kaveri felt uncomfortable telling Trina about picking out which house she would live in on the compound or how she would be traveling to Paris in a few months with Mackenzie. Trina was still scraping by with a shitty job at the Circle K in Frink. The change in Kaveri's circumstances had been so sudden and dramatic, she felt out of place connecting with her former life. Still, hers was a lonely existence with no friends her own age in Los Angeles.

She scrolled through the photos on her phone, lingering over the ones she and Trina had taken the previous Halloween, dressed up as vampires as they worked the same shift at the Circle K convenience store. On New Year's Eve, they had driven out to the desert and lit a campfire, tossing stones into the flames to represent all the things they wanted to leave behind in the coming year: the dead-end town of Frink, the fetid Salton Sea, and for Kaveri, living with her mom, Brittney, as a last resort after aging out of the foster care system. Afterward, they had climbed up on the big rock formations and shouted at the moon, like wild creatures. She smiled at the recollection of the fun they had, living in the wide-open, untamed desert flatlands.

Now, Mackenzie controlled her schedule and gently pushed her to live within the confines of her new life. Kaveri couldn't get a job but she could choose a charity to work for, provided it wasn't a messy or controversial cause. She couldn't join a gym where she would be susceptible to meeting people hoping to take advantage of her financially or otherwise. Kaveri always thought that having a lot of money meant people had a lot of options but now she felt how narrow her world had become. Kaveri impulsively dialed Trina's number but she was secretly relieved when it went to voicemail. She hung up without leaving a message. Gerte approached, her thick body moving like a machine, fleshy arms pumping, as she hurried across the lawn to the pool.

"Your grandmother needs to speak to you and Miss Sierra about something important," she ordered. It was not a request.

"Thank you, Gerte."

Kaveri stood and put her pool cover-up on, before following Gerte to the house. She felt like a child being called in to answer for breaking a crystal dish. She saw her mother, Sierra, arriving at the same time with a similar look on her face. When she stepped into the parlor, she saw the household staff assembled as well as the head gardener, Johan.

Mackenzie motioned her and Sierra to sit near her on the sofa, before standing and casting a cool, appraising look over the group. When she spoke, her voice betrayed no anxiety, only a stoic, steely sense of control.

"We had a visit today from some agents with the FBI. They

were asking questions about the family, about the return of my granddaughter, Kaveri. Someone with significant connections has instigated this, his identity is not important. We have our team of attorneys to take care of it. I want you all to be on your guard about people trying to speak to you, to get information about the family. Anyone who speaks to someone from law enforcement or the press will be terminated."

There was a shift among the employees, some looking to others for reassurance, some confused and frightened by the news. Sierra looked more intrigued than scared, a faint smile on her face. Kaveri was terrified. She had no idea what the FBI could want with her but she feared it had to do with the details of her new life that didn't quite add up, even to her. She doubted the reassurances that Rawley Jaynes and Brittney gave her when she questioned how she could be Kaveri Browne, the missing heiress. Now she knew she wasn't the only one.

Mackenzie was speaking quietly with the security team, while the rest of the staff resumed their work. Kaveri looked around the room and nothing felt right. It was all too perfect. She heard Trina's voice in her head, the words she had said to Kaveri when Rawley Jaynes first showed up in Frink.

"If it sounds too good to be true, Megan, it is!"

SIXTEEN

Emily and Ryan sat at a table in La Bruschetta, a classic Italian trattoria in Westwood, near their FBI office. They were navigating the Home at Last website, which listed Kaveri Browne and Danica Hansen as the latest success stories.

"When did Jaynes start this venture?" Emily asked.

"In the past two months. It seems to have come on the heels of finding Kaveri and Danica. It looks to me like the guy got the idea that he could turn these two cases into a full-time, lucrative gig. And like Zanie told me, they want ten thousand up front and they give no guarantee," Ryan said. "Imagine if you get ten desperate families willing to pay ten grand and they get no results? A hundred grand scam!"

"I think there's something to what Janelle said about how 'when she and Amber saw what was in it', they were on board for DNA," Emily said, skeptically, taking a sip of her double espresso.

"Maybe they meant that what was in it, was finding Danica after so long?" Ryan suggested but Emily gave him a jaded look.

"They weren't interested in that," she replied quietly.

"Are you sure? It's not like you know them personally, right?" Ryan asked, puzzled by her conviction. "You only met Amber Hansen today."

Emily shrugged, deflecting his inquiry. "You're right. I guess it's just my own bias, as a parent. Wondering how they could've done so little to find Danica."

Emily wished she could tell Ryan the truth about her identity, it would make the investigation much easier, but she couldn't. It wasn't that she didn't trust him, he had backed her up in the take-down of James Tibbs, putting his life and his career at risk. She knew it would be too big a burden for him to carry, and he was just beginning his career with the FBI, full of idealism.

"I think Jaynes agreed to give them a lot of money for... something," she said cautiously. Jaynes was lying about Shirelle Sanders' DNA test but she needed more proof.

"Does Jaynes look like he has a lot of cash to throw around? He looked pretty low rent to me," Ryan said.

"Maybe not Rawley Jaynes but who does he have a close relationship with who has a lot of money? Unlimited funds?" Emily asked.

Ryan nodded. "Mackenzie Browne. But why? She doesn't need to pay other people to go along with Jaynes and support the idea that he's some master investigator."

"Unless she does. And Kaveri is a fraud," Emily said, signaling the waiter for the check. Her phone rang; it was Stephanie at the FBI offices.

"Hi, Em, listen, I ran the plates on the Honda you saw at the Browne compound, they were previously registered to the family trust, but the car was pulled out and changed in the past few months to an address in Brentwood. It's a condo on Barrington Avenue; the owner is listed as Sierra Browne. It was purchased about four months ago, paid in cash. The car is in her name, also."

"Thanks, Steph," Emily replied, hanging up. "Sierra Browne seems to be setting herself up outside of the family compound. She bought a condo a few months ago and switched the registration on her car to her own name."

The waiter arrived and discreetly slid the check to Ryan, who tossed his credit card down.

"What're you doing? I'll put it on my expense account," Emily protested.

"And I can put it on mine just as easily. Can't a guy pay the tab with a pretty girl?" he asked, jokingly.

"Okay, the next one's on me. How's Erik, by the way," she asked.

"We split up. I moved to a new place," he said.

"I thought you guys were getting married?" she asked, surprised.

"So did I. But you know, he's an actor, he's very good-looking and he met some older producer guy who can do a lot more for him than a lowly FBI agent."

"No! I'm sorry to hear that. I thought you two sounded like the perfect couple."

"So did everyone, but what can you do? How're things with your family these days?"

Emily looked away. No one at work knew about her marital separation from Antonio.

"Fine," she lied.

"Must be nice, being in a long-term relationship with kids, knowing you've got that part of your life settled and figured out. I hope I get there one day. Right now, it's just keep moving forward and don't look back," Ryan said, staring into his espresso before swirling it and drinking it down in one final gulp. She could sense that he was carrying something heavy on his heart, perhaps things he wasn't able to talk about yet.

Emily smiled at him and patted his hand reassuringly.

"You're right. Just keep moving forward, and don't look back," she said.

Dolores followed Juli and Liza into the house, carrying a bag of groceries from Aldi. The girls ran in, dumped their backpacks and searched for the banana milk in the fridge.

"I'll make you some quesadillas and then get your homework done," Dolores said.

"We finished it in school," Liza said, too quickly.

"I'll check it to make sure," Dolores replied, raising one eyebrow. "Even the math sheet?"

Liza nodded, shifting her foot from one to the other.

Antonio padded through from the home office.

"Daddy! What're you doing home?" Juli asked.

"I had a ton of calculations to do, and I can do them from home so I left early," he said, with a smile, taking a carton of banana milk for himself.

"When did we start getting banana milk?" he asked.

Liza looked at him as if he had three heads. "Jungkook drinks it! God, Daddy. You're so cringey!"

"What does that mean?" he asked in surprise.

"Uncool, embarrassing. You're also kind of chopped," Juli said, seriously.

"And who is Jungkook? Is he a boy in your class?" he asked.

"GOD!! DAD!!" they both screeched, and ran from the room, giggling.

He looked to Dolores for help, but she shrugged. "I guess you don't pay attention to the posters in their room, do you? It's BTS, Toño. The Korean band."

"I didn't know, I thought they were just good-looking Asian guys."

"Well, Juli wanted a Jungkook bedspread with a big image of him half-dressed and Emily said no. So at least someone is paying attention," she said, turning away to unload the groceries.

Antonio was quiet for a moment, sensing her disappointment and anger with him.

Finally, he asked, "I know Emily may never forgive me, but do you think you will?"

She looked at him, and let out a heavy sigh. "Why did you do something so stupid, *mijo*? Why did you risk everything? Emily is not like that Anjelica Romero, desperate for a man and willing to look the other way and make excuses for you. She will divorce you if you can't fix this, you know that?"

He looked at his hands resting on the countertop and shook his head.

"I know. But I don't know how to fix it, she won't let me in at all. It's like she has a big wall up all around her."

"What did you expect? A girl who went through what she did as a child? She's a survivor and she knows when she must get away from danger, to shut down a threat. And that's what you've become for her."

A danger... a threat...

She could see in his face how her words had cut him to the core. It broke her heart. He had become the worst thing possible to the person he loved the most.

"What do I do if she can't get past it?" he asked, suddenly looking like the little boy Dolores had helped raise. She took his hand and looked him straight in the eye.

"You find a place to live with nice bedrooms for the girls. You get an attorney to work out all the details. You co-parent with Emily and you show up at every school event and music recital. You don't bring girlfriends over to spend the night when the girls are there. And since Emily has a huge inheritance, you do not take one penny from her or any property that belongs to her. If you do, I will never speak to you again, Toño."

SEVENTEEN

"Since Mackenzie Browne made it clear she's not cooperating with us, we need to speak to Kaveri alone or at the very least, the people she lived with when she was Megan Hoard." Emily and Ryan were sat across from SAC Powers in his office. "I would like to speak to Sierra Browne, to get her take on all of this, but getting to either of them is difficult. Mackenzie has a tight grip on the family."

Powers leaned back in his chair, his expression stoic and inscrutable.

"It's clear that Rawley Jaynes has been working for the family for years as a fixer of sorts," Ryan added. "He's probably broken the law to do it. I think we can guess that it was in exchange for significant amounts of money. The relationship with the Brownes raises doubts about Kaveri, at least to me."

Powers nodded. "I agree. Kaveri's return seems like a miracle, and I don't believe in miracles. We can walk this line a bit longer, it shouldn't take much time to get to the bottom of it. Let's see if we can get to it without needing to subpoena financials or other information."

"But if we need to?" Emily asked.

"We'll cross that bridge if we need to. I hope we won't," he said, nodding succinctly.

"We haven't yet discovered Senator Hubbard's connection to this, but given the history of allegations against him, I think he's going to float to the top, so to speak," Emily said.

"That's what trash usually does," Powers said dryly in a moment of uncharacteristic candor, before he caught himself and stood to signal the end of the meeting.

"Tomorrow we're going to go up to Frink to speak to the people who knew Kaveri as Megan Hoard, and we'll speak to the parents of Shirelle Sanders or I should say Danica Hansen. Danica's bio family seemed like grifters when I met them earlier today. So, there may be a money angle," Emily said.

"And I'll go as far as I can into Jaynes' new business operation, posing as Caleb Morgan," Ryan added.

"Good. Just try to keep everything on the quiet side as you proceed. We don't want to call any attention to this."

Emily and Ryan walked out of his office; once they were down the hall out of earshot, Ryan whispered, "What was that? Get to the bottom of it but we won't need subpoenas or warrants for records? Keep it quiet and don't attract attention when going after one of the richest families in the country? Why don't we just take the metro rail to Mars while we're at it?"

"I get the sense that Powers is in a tight spot as well. I don't think he wants to do this, but he feels he has to because it's a senator asking," Emily replied quietly.

"Yeah, but we don't work for politicians. We don't take an oath to protect senators, we swear to the constitution!" Ryan said, his anger bubbling up.

"Now who's being unrealistic? Like we don't do politically motivated things all the time?"

"I know. But what do you think Hubbard is after? Just your gut feeling?" Ryan asked.

"I don't know. Why would a seventy-six-year-old senator be worried about a twenty-year-old heiress suddenly showing up?"

"Maybe the key word is 'heiress.' Could Hubbard be in line to inherit something when Jinx dies? They are very close friends," Ryan suggested.

"Could be."

En route to their office, they found Stephanie buried in work at her desk. She waved at them, then handed each a file.

"I just printed this. I'll send over a digital copy as well. This file is the background on the other woman that Rawley Jaynes found, Danica Hansen. She's been living with Hilda and Roy Sanders in Baker since she was approximately nine or ten years old, which coincides with the age at which she disappeared. There is a record of her living with a cousin of Hilda Sanders, Coralee Buell, prior to living with them, but no idea for how long. There is a birth certificate for a Danica Hansen with her parents listed as Glenn and Amber Hansen but no birth certificate for Shirelle Sanders. Nothing under the name Shirelle Buell either, which probably means that the birth was never registered. Coralee Buell is a transient, no established address. She has never collected social security, even though she would've been eligible a few years ago so she seems to have disappeared."

"So, this ties into what Zanie said, that they work with birth certificates and other documents. What if they look for people who don't have a clear line of identification? Home births away from hospitals which keep detailed legal records," Emily suggested.

"My great grandmother told my mother that when she was little in Oklahoma, they'd only go to the government offices once every few years and they took all the kids together and had them registered on the same day. So, they all had the same birthday," Ryan said.

"And this Coralee Buell could've been involved in Danica Hansen's abduction if there's no record of her being Danica's biological mother. We know nothing about her. The whole thing's a mess," Stephanie said.

Emily said nothing and kept her eyes down, studying the pattern on the carpet.

"What do you think, Emily?" Ryan asked.

"It could be. Kids who get abducted or abandoned often don't have proper, legal paperwork to confirm their identity. That's why so many of them live at the margins of society. It's like a shadow world, far removed from what we consider normal. Their histories have blank pages," Emily replied quietly. "But the fact that Jaynes found Shirelle Sanders means he could've done the same thing for Kaveri Browne."

Stephanie turned back to her computer as they headed toward their office. Emily's nerves were raw. The pressure she felt, investigating the woman using her name, claiming her true identity, was unbearable. Theorizing over someone she knew was a fraud and being unable to tell the truth out loud, created such intense cognitive dissonance, she felt like she was going crazy.

She had been developing a headache for the past hour and now it was a pulsing pain at the base of her skull. She snapped the rubber band on her wrist several times, hoping the sting might help her reset. Seated in their office, surrounded by the whiteboard filled with notes and photographs, and files spread out on the conference table, Emily rested her head in her hands and said, "In the TV interview, Danica seemed nervous and uncertain. Almost like she didn't want to be there. She's socially awkward, she's not slick like Mackenzie."

"I felt bad for Danica, the way she kept looking to Jaynes for help. It's got to be a big mind-fuck, right? She said she was very happy with the Sanders and then suddenly her whole life is upended by Rawley Jaynes. It probably upset her, I mean, there doesn't seem to be any great benefit to being Danica Hansen, right?" Ryan said, popping open a can of Coke from the office fridge.

Unexpectedly, his words pierced Emily like a crossbow. Without knowing it, he had cut right to the raw center of who she had been at fifteen years old, and she still was at thirty-eight, a woman working tirelessly every day to outrun the girl she used to be. A girl who wasn't missed, who was never enough. In that moment it was as if Andy Ryan could see her, knew her better than anyone else.

There doesn't seem to be any great benefit to being Danica Hansen...

He was right. To be Danica Hansen was a liability. The part of her that remained unhealed, that was triggered by every step they took in the Kaveri Browne investigation, still had the power to push her to the brink of tears at random, inopportune moments. She kept her eyes on the files in front of her and nodded, afraid that her voice would break if she spoke.

Ryan noted the change in her and leaned in, gently touching her hand.

"Hey, Em, are you okay? Did I say something wrong?" he asked, quietly.

She shook her head and replied, "No, not at all... it's just... a lot of stuff comes up with these cases, you know?"

"I'm sorry. I have no idea how it would feel to have lived this. I say stupid things sometimes..." he apologized.

"You didn't do anything wrong, Andy. This is how it rears up, unexpectedly. I have other stuff going on also..." she hesitated, unsure how much to disclose.

"You're not sick, are you?" he asked. He looked at her with such raw concern and anxiety, she took his hand to reassure him.

"No, nothing like that. No one at work knows, but I'm... separated from my husband."

Ryan leaned back in his chair, in stunned surprise. "No way. I'm so sorry. What happened, if it's okay to ask?"

"Infidelity. On his part, not mine," she said, grabbing a tissue from a box on the table and wiping her eyes.

Now Ryan's expression turned hard; he looked like a guy about to get into a bar fight.

"Then he has something wrong with him. What kind of idiot screws up like that when he has you locked down, ring on your finger, with two kids? He may be a rocket scientist but he's a moron. Let's get out of here before I follow you home and give him a black eye."

Emily smiled, surprised at his shift to protective alpha male, but flattered. She'd made the right choice in Andy Ryan for her partner on this investigation. With the upheavals in her family life, it felt good to know that at least someone still had her back.

Louise Niedermeier sat up in her bed at the El Sol Memory Care facility. She heard something or she thought she did. Her studio apartment had a small balcony, but it was on the second floor, and no one could have climbed up onto it. She had been taking her afternoon nap and as the sun began its journey to the west, it cast shadows in her room. She swore she saw a figure waiting in the small bathroom, across from her wall closet. She pulled her blanket up to her neck, as if it were protective armor.

She'd been jumpy since the blond woman had asked her about the little girl. She hadn't thought of it in years. Of course not, they were not allowed to mention the little girl at the big house. Lucille had been the one to clear out her room and put her things in the big, top-floor attic with the locked door. She'd cried as she folded the little dresses and undergarments. Small, white cotton, like small handkerchiefs with snaps and buttons. She was so small when she went to the orchard.

Louise heard the noise again. She picked up her room phone and dialed the desk downstairs. It was answered by Valerie, the assistant director of services at El Sol.

"Hello, Louise, what can I do for you?"

"Hello, Valerie, can you send someone up to check my room? I think there's a person hiding in my bathroom!" Louise whispered, terrified.

"I think you're imagining it, Louise. Remember last month when you thought you heard someone singing in the hallway at night? You imagine a lot of things, dear," Valerie replied, impatiently.

"No, this is real! I saw a shadow and I've heard someone in there!" Louise insisted, feeling the panic swirling in her stomach.

"Okay, dear. I'll send someone up, okay?" Valerie sounded bored and distracted.

"Please, please hurry!" Louise whispered.

Louise lay back on her bed, the covers pulled up over her face, afraid to see the strange shadows. Someone from the staff would be here soon, it would be fine. She would just lie quiet until someone arrived. She never saw the figure slip quietly from her bathroom and move silently to her bed. Louise started when the pillow was held over her face, her frail body fighting back without the strength to stop her attacker until her body fell limp in death.

EIGHTEEN

Zanie paced back and forth in the living room of the home she shared with Rawley. He had been vaping weed nonstop ever since they'd learned about the FBI investigating Kaveri. She'd tried to stay busy by doing a basic search on Caleb and Callie Morton. She found his website and several companies that he had worked for and located his profile on several dating sites. But she couldn't find anything on Callie or her disappearance. No records of any kind for her. There was no mention of her in the local Boulder newspapers or social media accounts. There was no public record of her birth. Callie Morgan was a complete blank.

Zanie had the sinking feeling that Caleb Morgan might not have been real. He could have been an undercover agent, and she had told him about the ten-thousand-dollar retainer and checking birth certificates to verify victims. She assured herself that none of that meant anything, but she knew that with just the tiniest sliver of information, the FBI could unravel everything. She had to get out in front of any trouble that might come for them. She dialed Danica.

"Hello, Zanie," Danica said. "I'm on a break at work so I can't talk much."

"That's fine, honey. I just wanted to let you know that two FBI agents have been looking into Kaveri Browne and they might contact you to ask about Rawley and everything. You don't have to talk to them, okay? It's better if you don't."

"FBI agents? That sounds serious," Danica said.

"It's not. It's just routine, honey. Kaveri's family is very prominent, so this type of thing happens sometimes. But don't talk to the FBI at all, about anything, all right?" Zanie tried to sound casual.

"Okay. I won't. Thanks for letting me know. I have to get back," Danica said hurriedly, hanging up.

Zanie breathed a sigh of relief. If Mackenzie kept Kaveri under control, everything would blow over. But she was angry at Mackenzie, who'd kept Rawley like a dog on a leash with money and perks for so many years. And now when she needed his help the most, Mackenzie held back information that had put them in the cross hairs of a U.S. senator. Maybe she should make a break from all of it and start afresh with no dirty money and underhanded shenanigans. But that was the only world Rawley knew and if she left him, she'd be single again. Being with a con man wasn't perfect but it was better than being alone.

By the time Emily arrived home, dinner was over, and the house was quiet. She opened the big electric gate and pulled her car into the driveway. An illuminated Santa and his reindeer welcomed her, and she saw that Dolores must've had the gardener put up the multi-colored exterior house lights. She hoped everyone was asleep and she'd be able to grab a quick bite from the fridge before going to bed.

When she walked in the front door, Moose greeted her and she saw that Antonio was in the den, watching television. When he heard her footsteps, he jumped up to meet her.

"How was it today?" he asked.

"It was fine, same way it always is. It's an investigation," she said, dropping her briefcase and slipping out of her shoes. She felt a flash of remorse for being so short with him, but she didn't have the energy for the niceties and considerations that they used to share. She was tired and her nerves were shot to hell. She moved to the fridge and opened it to peer inside.

"Dolores saved you a plate. She made chicken enchiladas," he said, leaning on the counter and refilling his glass of wine. "Want me to pour you a glass?"

She shook her head. "No, I'm working. The house looks nice from the outside."

"Yeah, it does," he said, taking a long sip of Cabernet. "Can we talk about this, Em?"

"About what?" she asked, wearily.

"About us, all of this. What we're doing."

"We're separated while we figure out if this marriage can be saved. I'm sorry if it's not resolving fast enough for you but you can't push a river."

"I've made it clear that I definitely want to save it," he said, decisively, setting his jaw and laying his palms on the counter, as if ready for a negotiation.

"And I've told you that I'm not sure. Just because you've made your mind up, doesn't mean I owe you an answer right now," she replied, putting her plate of food into the microwave.

"It's been almost six months, Emily."

"And we've been married for thirteen years so six short months is not a long time in the big picture, is it?" She knew that her lingering anger was raw but she didn't try to hide it. She had stopped caring about protecting his feelings.

"I'm doing well in therapy; I've got a better understanding of how I put myself in that situation with Anjelica..." he explained, but Emily cut him off.

"Have you been in touch with her?" she asked, reaching for cutlery to avoid his gaze. "I told you to see her again, you need to figure out if that is what you really want."

"No, she is not what I want! I don't need to see her again to know that," he said, running his hands through his hair in frustration. "When we got back from Arrowhead, I called her and told her that the whole thing was a mistake, and I was sorry. And it was over."

"Just like that?" she asked, with a caustic chuckle.

He sat in silence, his arms crossed protectively.

"Lydia says I should take all the time I need to figure out how I feel. And I'll know at some point if I can do this or not. I hate who this has turned me into, but I can't seem to force myself to feel any differently than I do," Emily said, feeling helpless against a tsunami of conflicted emotions.

"You can try," he suggested, cautiously.

"Like I haven't tried? To bend and force myself to forgive and get past it? My entire life is a never-ending exercise in getting past things! I can't change what James Tibbs did but maybe I don't need any more things that I have to get past? Maybe I don't have any more 'getting past it' left in me!"

He nodded, backing off. He rinsed his wine glass in the sink and turned to her.

"Okay. We'll talk about it another time. I'm sure it was a long day."

She watched him go, her heart and mind caught in a tumble of contradictions. Part of her wanted him to be the easy, comforting presence he used to be but their estrangement had made him edgy and uncertain, every conversation felt loaded with his expectations for a reconciliation. She knew he thought she was punishing him for his affair with Anjelica, but she wasn't. Punishment would've been easy and it would've ended by now. What she felt was something more complicated and fundamental. It was the painful sense that there was a part of him that she had never seen, never known. A part of him that would risk their family life for easy ego gratification and when she saw him that way, he was a stranger to her.

She looked at the plate of food and realized her appetite was gone. She washed it down the garbage disposal and went upstairs to take a quick shower, Moose following her diligently to his plushy bed in her room. Afterward she went to check on her daughters to find their beds empty. Her heart lurched in knee-jerk panic, and she hurried back to the bedroom where she found them both under her covers, fast asleep and waiting for her. She climbed in between them, breathing in the scent of their freshly washed hair. She wrapped her arms around their small, warm bodies, clad in soft cotton pajamas, and closed her eyes, feeling a sense of peace come over her.

Anjelica Romero drove her Toyota Camry along the winding streets of La Cañada, taking in the huge, impressive homes and pristine landscapes behind iron fences. She had checked into the Airbnb in Montrose a few hours earlier and enjoyed a nice dinner at a restaurant on Foothill Boulevard.

She'd been calling and texting Antonio for the past few months and he hadn't responded. She knew he'd told her that their relationship was a mistake and had no future, that he would never leave his wife, who he loved and respected, but she didn't believe him. If he loved and respected her, why had he flirted outrageously with Anjelica at the reunion in Arizona? Why had he left his kids with the aunties so they could sneak off and spend time alone together? And why had he made love to her in her own bed, with his kids in the next room?

She knew better. He was afraid of losing the respect of the family, of his friends and colleagues. He wanted the attention that she could give him, that his wife was too busy for. But like most men, he had to test the waters first; they never took any great leap without knowing they had a soft place to land. He needed to be reminded that she was ready and waiting for him.

She saw that he had a nice, comfortable life there in La Cañada. His work was close by, between his salary and his wife's they could afford to live in that big sprawling house, and he didn't want to lose it all. If they divorced, he would get half the value of the home and that would be several million dollars, easily enough for him and Anjelica to set up a life together. If he transferred to

Arizona, they could buy a mansion and have a whole new beginning, in more ways than one.

She parked her car underneath a tall pepper tree, its pendulous branches thick with red peppercorns. The sharp, pungent scent carried as she rolled her window down and relaxed back into her car seat. The house looked so pretty with the twinkling Christmas lights. Maybe Antonio would keep it in the divorce, and it would become their home together. She smiled at that thought; she'd always liked California.

NINETEEN

Emily pulled her car up to the school drop off and Liza and Juli clambered out, carrying their big backpacks and BTS Bento lunchboxes.

"Remember, Mommy has to be away overnight for a case but I'll call you around dinner time so you can fill me in on what happened today," she said.

"Okay! Catch the bad guys, Mommy," Liza said.

"And bring us a souvenir from wherever you're going to," Juli insisted.

Emily blew them a kiss. She pulled out of the busy drop-off area unaware that there were two people watching her. Anjelica Romero had been waiting outside the house, watching for Emily's car as it pulled out with Juli and Liza in the backseat. She wanted to get familiar with the family routines, the route to school, how the drop off worked. She hoped to be playing her part in all of it soon.

Norayr Apelian had parked up the block, keeping an eye out for the car that Zanie had described to him, after Mackenzie sent her a security photo of it at the compound. He stayed several cars behind Emily's Mercedes and had discreetly parked at the school when she arrived there, drinking down the remainder of his large McDonald's black coffee. When Emily left the school parking lot, he followed. He liked surveillance, the power of being the unseen eyes, watching everything someone did and where they went, completely oblivious to his presence. Even more, he enjoyed that the pretty, blond Emily Ray had no idea she had become the prey.

Emily was pulling onto the freeway when she called Ryan to coordinate the day's schedule. The night before had been so emotional and heavy, they had left without a plan.

"Hi, Em! Where do you want to meet up first?" Ryan asked upon answering.

"I'm going to check in on Louise Niedermeier and then I'll make a stop by the Burbank Studios where they film *The World Today* and see what I can find. So, let's meet at the studios in an hour," she said.

They also needed to make the three-hour trip to Frink, near the Salton Sea to interview Kaveri's former family and friends. They were booked to stay overnight in The Motel by The Sea and return the next day. Emily hoped that talking with the people who knew Kaveri when she was Megan Hoard might help them come to a conclusion about her legitimacy for SAC Powers and they could close the door on the whole unofficial investigation.

Emily arrived at the El Sol Memory Care facility and her heart quickened to find a large fire truck parked and an ambulance pulling away. She texted her dad and was relieved when he responded that he was in a yoga stretch class in the fitness studio. As she went inside, some of the residents were huddled in the foyer.

At the main desk, she spoke to a flustered desk attendant. "I'm here to visit Louise Niedermeier."

The attendant blanched and asked, "Are you a family member? We don't have any family members in her file."

"No, I'm an acquaintance of hers. My father, Michael Ray, lives here."

"I'm so sorry to tell you... but Louise died last night," the attendant replied, his shock was obvious. Emily stared at him, uncomprehending for a beat. She could see Louise clearly in her memory, her smile and frail hands reaching out to take Emily's just days prior.

"She died? I just spoke to her the other day. She didn't seem close to death at all," Emily said.

"You know, at this age it can be anything that takes them. She seemed fine but she didn't come down to dinner last night and we thought she was feeling tired. But then she missed breakfast too and we went into her apartment and found her."

Emily stepped back, as she saw the paramedics leave with an empty stretcher. The mortuary workers would arrive soon to take the body. Emily knew there was more that Louise wanted to tell her about Kaveri, she'd seen it in the old woman's eyes when they met.

"Since Louise has no family on file, who is the emergency contact for her?" Emily asked.

The attendant looked on his computer and said, "It's the Doucette-Browne Family Trust. They pay the bills and are taking care of the funeral plans."

Half an hour later, Emily was at the gate of Burbank Studios, still pondering over Louise Niedermeier's death. She had been bright-eyed, laughing and chatting with her tablemates at El Sol after the movie. Emily noticed that she had eaten all of her dessert before the attendant had come to wheel her back to her room. Emily knew that if she made any inquiries of the Doucette-Browne estate, there would be no response.

Emily showed her badge to the security guard at Burbank Studios, who had called the production office for *The World Today* to get clearance to let her in. He waved her forward and she drove onto the lot, following a confusing map to Stage Six and the adjoining offices. She parked and wandered into the big open door of the sound stage, with its high scaffolds and cat walks with lights hanging overhead. The familiar newsroom sets looked flimsy up close, like an empty playhouse waiting for people to bring it to life.

A harried, nervous production assistant approached her. "Excuse me, can I help you? I'm Anica. One of the PAs."

Emily flashed her badge and said, "Special Agent Emily Ray of the FBI. I'd like to speak to the staff who worked on the episode of *The World Today*, featuring Kaveri Miller Browne?"

Anica drew back, her eyes wide. "The FBI? I thought the guard at the gate was joking!"

Emily smiled. "No, the FBI doesn't joke around too much."

Anica laughed nervously. "Sure. Why don't you come with me to see the producer and Jasmin Lourdes is here also, going over the stories for tonight."

Emily followed her to a nearby low-slung stucco building that housed the offices for *The World Today*.

"If you'll wait here, I'll let them know. Do you want a bottle of water or anything?" Anica asked.

"No, I'm fine," Emily said.

A moment later, a tall, athletic woman stepped out of her office, dressed in a stylish Donna Karan suit, her silver hair cut into a pixie style.

"Special Agent Ray? I'm the executive producer, Elinor Buckley. How can I be of help to you?"

"I have a few questions about your segment on Kaveri Browne. Could we speak in your office?" Emily asked.

Elinor led her in and closed the door behind them. Anica waited in the outer office, exchanging concerned glances with Elinor's assistant.

"What would you like to discuss, Agent Ray?" Elinor asked, with a flat smile.

"How did your program vet Rawley Jaynes' claims, regarding his two clients? He explained his process of tracking them down, which was vague and inconclusive since we engage in these types of investigations regularly in the FBI. How did you verify that his claims were true?"

"Well, we didn't need to verify them because they all had positive DNA matches to their families," Elinor explained.

"Did you verify both with independent labs?"

Elinor looked at her, confused. "We didn't feel we needed to. Once the families verify that the DNA is a match, why would we question them?"

"Did you speak to any of Kaveri's previous family or friends?"

"No, Mr. Jaynes and Ms. Miller Browne said that was not necessary and would cause more problems, since it was a big adjustment for Kaveri."

"And was there a reason you didn't include the Hansen family in your segment?" Emily asked.

Elinor's smile evaporated. "Danica didn't want her real mother or aunt to be involved. I gather the whole thing is difficult for the Sanders, who had no idea that she was an abducted child before she came to live with them."

Emily's phone beeped with a message from Ryan.

I'm here, outside the studio gates

"Thank you, Ms. Buckley. If we need anything else we'll be in touch," Emily said, pushing her phone back into her pocket.

"I mean, we do due diligence on our segments. We don't just accept what people tell us but when someone like Mackenzie Miller Browne agrees to do a segment—"

Emily interrupted her, "You just accept what she tells you."

As Emily followed the map back to her car, Anica trotted up behind her and tapped her arm.

"Excuse me, I need to talk to you," Anica whispered.

Emily turned to her. "What is it?"

Anica looked over her shoulder, anxiously. "I could get fired for this, but we've been getting calls from a woman who knew Kaveri Browne as a child. She says they grew up together since infancy and she always lived with her mother, Brittney."

"Did she leave her name?"

"No, she sounded kind of scared. I told Ms. Buckley and even Jasmin but they told me not to talk to her. They just want to bury this, so the show doesn't look bad. I thought you should know," Anica said, before hurrying back to the office.

Outside the studio gates, Emily found Ryan waiting for her.

"Louise Niedermeier died last night. The Browne family was paying her expenses at El Sol," she told him.

"She died?" Ryan asked, surprised. "Do you think it was a coincidence? You said she was quite old, right?"

"Maybe. But I sensed that she wanted to tell me more. Her attendant insisted she went back to her apartment. She was bright-eyed and smiling. Now she's dead."

"I admit, it looks too convenient."

"And someone called *The World Today* to tell them that she knew Kaveri since she was a baby and the story they told on TV isn't true."

"What? Who is it and how do we talk to her?"

"She didn't leave a name but there's only one place to find her. We have to get to Frink, ASAP."

Bernila Domingo stood in the hallway outside the activities room, watching as the Smith Brothers Mortuary staff wheeled Louise Niedermeier's body out to their waiting van. This type of thing happened regularly at places like El Sol Memory Care. Elderly people were dying all the time and no one thought anything of it. They had sudden strokes, silent heart attacks or aneurisms in the solitude of their bedrooms, only to be discovered later.

Louise had been sharp enough to make that call to the main desk but luckily, no one came to follow up on her fears. Bernila had been fortunate that Valerie was at the desk; she didn't give a hoot about the residents. She resented them so there was no way she was going to send someone up to check on Louise. It had been so easy. The old woman didn't even have much fight in her, at her age.

It was lucky Bernila had received the call from The Money Lady, who paid the bills. Bernila didn't even know her name; she was just The Money Lady. She always gave Bernila a little extra to keep a close eye on Louise but when the daughter of Mr. Ray started asking Louise questions and Louise started talking, Bernila knew to take care of it. She'd received quite a big bonus in her bank account within an hour.

It didn't really matter anyway. Louise had no family, no children or grandkids to mourn her. As far as Bernila knew, she'd come over from Germany as a young woman and spent her whole life as a maid for a rich family. She never had visitors, except for another old German lady who came a few times. Louise was going to die soon, anyway. What did it matter if Bernila just helped her along her way a little earlier?

TWENTY

Mackenzie stood inside Sierra's kitchen, filled with bottles brewing homemade kombucha, and flats growing wheat grass. Sierra was preparing a poultice of castor oil and herbs to use for a lingering headache that had been plaguing her in recent days. Mackenzie rolled her eyes as her daughter poured a strange-smelling concoction through a strainer into a glass bowl.

"What is this for, exactly?" She kept her distance; the smell was unpleasant.

"I already told you. It's an herbal treatment that should get rid of this pain in my head," Sierra said.

"Why don't you just take Tylenol or Advil?" Mackenzie asked, feeling the exasperation in her voice.

"And destroy my liver? No thanks, Mom," Sierra said, with an edge to her voice.

Mackenzie shrugged. Sierra was a bother, always following some crazy holistic guru or making her life more complicated when she could easily have taken a pill from the local drugstore. Mackenzie found it ridiculous that after so many years of drug use, now Sierra was all about living clean and free of chemicals and processed food. Mackenzie had a medicine chest filled with all manner of prescriptions to manage her life when it got difficult: anti-anxiety meds, muscle relaxers, high-octane painkillers to escape any discomfort. Nothing could ever be easy with Sierra. Mackenzie was already stressed, waiting for an update from Zanie about Emily Ray and Andy Ryan.

"What is it you wanted to see me about?" Mackenzie asked.

Sierra turned to her, wiping her hands on a towel. "I want to know what you want from Kaveri?"

Mackenzie was surprised at her daughter's astute observation but waved her off. "What do I want? Nothing but for her to take her place in the family now that she's back."

Sierra fixed her with a sardonic stare. "I know you, Mom. There's something you want from her. She wouldn't be here, otherwise."

Mackenzie felt anger rising within. "What nonsense are you saying? Your daughter is back; you should be happy and relieved. Instead, you're suspecting me of what? Some Machiavellian scheme? What could I possibly want from a twenty-year-old girl?"

"That's what I'm asking you."

"Jesus, Sierra. Have you been taking the medication that Dr. Nassif gave you?"

"Yeah. It's right here," Sierra said, taking a bottle from the cupboard and handing it to her. Mackenzie opened it and counted out the pills.

"Don't skip your dose. Otherwise, you'll get all confused again," Mackenzie advised.

"I'm not crazy, Mom," Sierra said quietly. "Kaveri is young I don't want you ruining her life."

"Please. Without me, this family would've capsized into ruin years ago. Sierra, just listen to me and stop letting insane ideas fill your head. Trust that I'm managing everything and protecting your best interests," Mackenzie said sharply, and left Sierra to her weird concoctions.

Sierra watched her go, trying hard to recall a single moment in her life when Mackenzie had done anything in her best interests. As usual, her mother had evaded answering her question, but she would get to the bottom of it. She knew from experience that when Mackenzie was in pursuit of a goal, things could become dangerous or spin out of control very quickly. She had Kaveri to think of now. She needed answers before she executed her escape from the toxic ash heap that her family had become. And a way to bring Kaveri with her.

Norayr called Zanie with an update as he discreetly followed Emily Ray's car, traveling on the 10 Freeway to the Salton Sea.

"Yes, any updates?" Zanie asked, anxiously.

"Mr. Ryan was home all evening. Ms. Ray left early today to take her children to school. Then she went to a retirement home for elderly people. Then to the Burbank Studios and now she's with Mr. Ryan, driving toward the high desert."

Zanie flinched when she heard "Burbank Studios," hoping nothing had come of it. She had to give Mackenzie an update, but she wanted answers of her own. Like why Harry Hubbard had put the FBI onto them.

"Stay on it and keep me posted on everything that happens. Every place she goes, who she talks to, all of it," Zanie said, hanging up as Rawley emerged from the bedroom, his eyes bloodshot.

"What's up?" he asked.

"I see you're finally up and awake," Zanie sniped at him.

"Call Mackenzie," he demanded.

"I was about to, Norayr is tailing them now. They're on the Ten Freeway—"

"CALL MACKENZIE!" he shouted, and Zanie jumped. She dialed the number with shaking hands. She had never seen this side of Rawley, and it scared her. He grabbed the phone.

"Hey, Mack, it's me. There's more to this than I knew so you handle it, get that fucking FBI agent off my back or I'll talk, understood? Same with that pansy-ass senator. Your problems have become my problems, and I don't want them. I'm ready to go scorched earth on everyone, got it?" he barked into the phone before slamming it down.

"Next time Norayr checks in, I'm talking to him," Rawley said, wiping the sweat from his upper lip.

Zanie approached him, taking his hand.

"Babe, why don't we just let this go? Forget about Mackenzie, she has what she wanted. We could just move on to something new and forget the whole plan, right? This is getting too messy. I haven't even told my sister yet and she's going to freak out," she said.

"I don't care what your pain-in-the-ass sister thinks. We can't forget anything until the FBI is done with it. This shit will just follow us."

"I'm just... kinda worried. I haven't heard back from Caleb Morgan, and I can't find any record of his missing sister, Callie. Nothing. I'm worried that he might not have been... legit," she admitted, tentatively.

Rawley focused his bleary eyes on her. "What did you say? You think he might not have been legit?"

Now Zanie chattered away like a magpie. "I mean, we didn't know about the FBI when I met him, and he asked questions. I'm wondering if he might have been undercover or something."

Rawley felt a rage bursting from his solar plexus, and he grabbed her by the neck, easily lifting her off the ground.

"You gave him details of how we work and now you think he might be an FBI agent, you stupid bitch?" he screamed as she squirmed against his grip.

"Rawley... let... go... I can't... breathe..." she struggled to speak.

He shook her violently and tossed her to the floor where she hit her head with a heavy thud. He rubbed his eyes and went to the bathroom to splash water on his face. His head was throbbing. He opened the Xanax bottle and took two pills, dry, then went back to Zanie and knelt beside her.

"Okay. I'm sorry, babe. I just lost it for a minute. It's over now.

I'll handle the stuff that Norayr is doing. You gotta do a job yourself if you want it done right," he said, touching her hair. She didn't move and his hand felt wet. He rolled her over and recoiled at the sight of her open eyes, flat and expressionless. There was a dark red stain spreading on the white tile floor. Zanie Lichtman was dead.

TWENTY-ONE

Kaveri drove her new BMW X5 up Wilshire Boulevard, toward home. She and Mackenzie had been to the dealership earlier in Beverly Hills to pick it up. Kaveri had chosen the royal blue X5 with the gray leather interior. When the salesman handed her the keys, she almost fainted. She'd never even owned a car before, let alone a luxury ride like this one. Mackenzie told her to drive back home to the compound as she had an appointment with the family lawyers.

Kaveri paired her iPhone with the car's Bluetooth and put on her favorite Spotify station. The speakers were so amazing, she laughed out loud, banging her hands on the steering wheel in exhilaration. She was so excited, she asked Siri to call Trina back home in Frink.

"Hey, Megan! What's up, girl?" Trina's chirpy voice answered in one ring.

"Bruh! You gotta call me Kaveri now!"

"Sorry. I forget. What's going on?"

"I just got a car! It is fire! A BMW!" Kaveri shrieked.

"When are you driving it up here to see me?"

"I don't know..." Kaveri felt her heart sink. "I've got to get permission," she mumbled.

"Why? You're twenty years old, not twelve. We could cruise to Palm Springs!"

Kaveri smiled at the thought of the two of them driving along, with her American Express card in her wallet, able to stay in any hotel they wanted.

"That'd be cool. But I still have to get permission. Everything here is kind of... different. Like my grandma's really careful and suspicious of everything and everyone."

"Maybe she's afraid someone will kidnap you for ransom." Trina laughed.

Kaveri turned up Beverly Glen to head back. As soon as she approached home, photographers started following her, snapping photos at red lights.

"I'll figure it out and we'll make some fun plan to hang out," Kaveri said with false optimism.

As the houses became bigger and the gates became taller, she felt like stepping back into her life with Trina and her other friends from home, would never happen. Or be allowed. Kaveri hung up as she pulled into the compound. She drove the path toward the quadrangle of homes and as she passed Sierra's house she saw her in the front yard, cutting flowers. Impulsively, Kaveri pulled into Sierra's driveway, eager to show her the new car.

"Hi, Mom!" Kaveri said, with a wave as she stepped out, trying to get more accustomed to referring to her that way.

Sierra froze for a moment, then her posture relaxed and she moved to Kaveri.

"Wow! This is a beauty!" Sierra exclaimed, walking around the BMW.

"I can't believe it! Do you want to go out for a spin?" Kaveri asked, suddenly.

Sierra knew an opportunity when it presented itself. "Sure! I'd love to!"

Kaveri got in and Sierra settled into the plush leather of the passenger's seat. Kaveri pulled the car out of the driveway and cruised past the guard gate, onto the wide streets of Holmby Hills. She looked nervously in her rearview mirror at the paparazzi.

"Don't they ever go away?" she asked.

"Take a right on this street and then cut down a little alleyway on the left. There's a way to ditch them," Sierra said.

Kaveri followed her instructions and soon they were on a quiet residential street, with no one after them. As they drove past a small park, Sierra tugged at Kaveri's arm and exclaimed, "Look at those beautiful flowers! Let's stop and get a photo."

Kaveri pulled into the parking lot and Sierra put a warning finger to her lips. Kaveri looked at her, puzzled, as Sierra stepped out of the car. Kaveri followed her onto a grassy knoll.

"Why are we being quiet?" Kaveri asked.

"Because I'm sure there are microphones hidden in your new car."

"Microphones?" Kaveri asked, horrified.

Sierra nodded. "I'm sure there are. Mackenzie has to know everything you're doing, thinking, who you're talking to. When did you choose the car?"

"Yesterday."

"And why didn't you drive it off the lot yesterday?"

"Because Mackenzie said they had to do a maintenance check before I could take it."

"A maintenance check on a brand-new car?" Sierra asked.

"Yes, you're right, that does seem a little strange," Kaveri replied, unsure. Mackenzie had told her Sierra had mental health problems.

Sierra stared at her for a long beat then said, "You think I'm crazy, that's what she told you, right? If you don't believe me, let's check the car. Just stay quiet and don't start the engine, it may activate everything. C'mon."

She led Kaveri back to the car and they unlocked the doors. Sierra slid herself flat across the passenger seat and ran her hand underneath it. She felt a small dial, affixed to the metal frame. She shone the flashlight on her phone underneath it and saw the small, black microphone. She gestured for Kaveri to come and see it and when she did, Kaveri looked to Sierra, her green eyes wide with fear.

Sierra signaled for her to remain quiet while she checked out the rest of the car, discovering two more microphones. They stepped away from the BMW and Sierra checked the undercarriage where she saw the blinking red light of a tracking device. When Kaveri saw it, she felt nauseous.

The two women walked into the park, along the garden path. Kaveri kept glancing back, anxious that someone was following them.

"But why would she do that? It's so creepy and weird!" Kaveri asked.

"Because my mother is a control freak and she always has some agenda that you don't know about. She wants something from you. I don't know what it is, but it has nothing to do with your well-being. She's a manipulative narcissist and you have to be careful with her," Sierra said.

"Do you think she might have put a camera in there also? To spy on me?"

"Maybe, you have to assume she probably has. Don't remove the microphones or the tracking device. Just take the tracker off and deactivate it if you don't want her to know where you are and you can put it back afterward. That way she'll think it just lost the signal temporarily. And know she can hear everything you say."

Dread swirled in Kaveri's stomach, her mind racing. The tensions with Mackenzie and Rawley Jaynes... Sierra constantly on guard, Gerte's odd demeanor and the decrepit old man in the big house, who cast a long shadow over all of them... all of it was off. Who could she trust?

"Did you see the FBI people that were at the house?" Kaveri asked.

"Yeah. They were asking about you. I was listening from the hallway. That's why my mother put everyone on lockdown. The Doucette-Browne code of silence."

"But I haven't done anything wrong! What does the FBI want with me?" Kaveri replied, her heart beating in fear.

"Of course you haven't. It's something she has done that put her on the FBI's radar. I wish I had known, I would have found a way to talk with them."

"There's a card from them in the desk in the tearoom. I looked in there and saw it," Kaveri said.

"Try to take a photo of it with your phone, so she won't see it missing. We should have a way to contact them if we need to."

Kaveri's voice caught in her throat. "Why would we need to contact them?"

Sierra took Kaveri's other hand in hers and looked directly into her eyes.

"Because people in this family are capable of anything to get what they want. And sometimes it's hard to know what that is. My grandfather is a horrible man. My mother is..." she considered for a long moment before continuing, "a vengeful, bitter woman who needs to control everyone around her."

"Then why do you stay?"

Sierra's eyes softened and she smiled sadly. "I did a lot of damage to myself trying to run away from them and figure out who I was. I'm building my courage up to leave and get free of them. And I don't plan on leaving you behind, sweetheart."

As they climbed back into the car, Kaveri realized that Sierra had called her "sweetheart," the way a normal mom would. It was the first time in her life someone had said that to her in kindness.

TWENTY-TWO

Dolores pulled out of the McDonald's on Foothill Boulevard while Juli and Liza enjoyed two soft serve ice-cream cones as an after-school treat. Emily would be away overnight, and Antonio was coming home early to take them all out for Thai food. She was glad she and Antonio had spoken honestly about what was going on with Emily. All she wanted was for them to work it out and keep the family together.

She turned onto their street and pulled up to the house to find a woman leaning against the front gate. She wore black leggings and a long burgundy sweater, her dark hair falling loose around her shoulders. When the woman saw Dolores, she smiled, and Dolores' heart dropped to her stomach. It was Anjelica Romero. When the twins saw her, they waved and called out.

"Dolores! Look, it's Cousin Angel from Arizona!"

Dolores opened the gate silently, and Anjelica followed her into the front yard.

"What brings you to Los Angeles, Anjelica?" Dolores asked, trying to keep her voice civil, as the girls ran to greet her.

"I had some people to visit and business to take care of," Anjelica said casually, hugging Juli and Liza. Dolores fought the urge to pull her hands off the little girls.

"Does Antonio know you're here?"

Anjelica smiled, her even white teeth flashing in the afternoon sun. "He will now!"

Dolores brought her inside, grateful that Emily wasn't home and that she would be gone for the evening. Moose approached cautiously, unsure about the new visitor. He sniffed her then backed up and began to bark.

"C'mon, big boy, let's go outside," Juli said, leading him to the door and pushing him into the yard.

As Anjelica cast an appraising eye on the luxurious interior of the house, Dolores filled the tea kettle, her hands shaking with fury.

"Would you like some tea or coffee?" she asked politely.

"Tea would be great, thank you, Tia," Anjelica said.

Dolores wanted to snap her head off for calling her "Tia," but she controlled her temper. She couldn't let the girls see that she was upset. She noticed that Anjelica's slender physique had filled out under her sweater; her face was fuller and her dimples more pronounced. In a sudden moment of clarity, she dropped a teacup in the sink, and it shattered.

She turned to Anjelica. "You've put on a bit of weight, haven't you?"

Anjelica gave her a knowing wink and smiled like the cat with a fat, yellow canary in its mouth.

"Yes, I have. I'm six months pregnant."

Juli and Liza let out a whoop and hugged her.

"A baby! Angel's having a baby!" Juli shouted.

Dolores stared at her, realizing her hope that Emily and Antonio would patch things up was a naïve fantasy. Their trouble was just beginning.

Emily and Ryan drove the 10 Freeway east toward the Salton Sea, the landscape becoming more flat and desolate with each passing mile. Emily had been uncharacteristically quiet for the past forty-five minutes.

"What's on your mind?" Ryan asked, finally.

"I'm wondering if I put Louise in danger by visiting her and asking about Kaveri. If the Brownes had something to do with her death to keep her quiet," Emily said quietly. "My dad lives there. It's just... scary."

"Or she might have died from something that had nothing to do with you. People that age can just go suddenly. It happened to my grandma that way," Ryan reassured her.

"And I'm thinking about DNA," Emily added.

"You think Kaveri's DNA test was false? Or rigged somehow? I mean, DNA is definitive."

"Legally, yes. But this isn't an investigation brought by the state or any other legal entity. It's a totally private matter; there's no official oversight to the DNA results. No judge, no lawyers, no police. These people can say whatever they want, and privacy laws protect them. If this were a real investigation, not some strange favor for Powers, we could have legal verification, but we don't."

"You think they're lying about the DNA?" Ryan asked.

"Possibly. Maybe it's been manipulated to give them the result they want. There are all kinds of rogue operators out there and with AI, anything can be fabricated."

They approached the Cabazon Dinosaurs, a roadside attraction featuring concrete and steel dinosaurs, right off the freeway in the middle of the desert landscape.

"What the hell is that?" Ryan asked.

"You've never heard of the Cabazon Dinosaurs? One of the weirdest things in California?" Emily laughed. "About a hundred of them all concrete, in the middle of bum-fuck nowhere. This part of the desert is full of stuff like that. Wait till you see Salvation Mountain!"

As they drove past, Ryan glared suspiciously at the big structures standing in the middle of the flat, sandy terrain, as if he were afraid they might start moving. Once they receded from view he turned back to Emily.

"So, if we flip the story and assume that Jaynes' discoveries are not legit, then Kaveri and Danica are involved in his con?" Ryan asked.

"I don't know. They could be victims of it. But the question is, why do it? What's the upside? If it's a con, who gains from it?" Emily pondered, turning over possibilities. If they looked at it from a different perspective, it might make sense. And if she could put enough pieces together, maybe she'd be able to solve it without bringing Danica Hansen into it. More than anything, she dreaded that interview and everything it would dredge up in her.

She sat up suddenly. "Remember how Ken Carlisle said that he figured that Jaynes found Kaveri because 'he had to'? And Ellis said that Jaynes is their fixer who delivers whatever they ask for? What if there's something related to the Doucette-Browne estate that requires Kaveri to be part of it? And it's important now because Jinx is close to death? What if it's all about money for all of them? Even Harry Hubbard? What if he needs a ton of money to make something go away?"

"Okay, so we need the trust documents to see what the specific provisions are for the money. And if Kaveri is part of it, then we work from the angle that the kid is a fake?"

"Maybe. And Danica could be part of it to bolster the idea that Kaveri is legitimate. To show that Jaynes has done it more than once, right?" Emily said.

"But that's a big reach. Say he finds a candidate to be Kaveri. She has a lot to gain, a big family fortune. But how does he find other people to go along with the same type of thing? They're not inheriting millions of dollars," Ryan said, skeptically.

"Right. But like you said, people will do strange things for money. And if we follow it, the money usually leads us to the right place."

"We're going to need to pull bank statements and those trust documents. But I don't know how we're going to do that without subpoenas," Ryan said.

"Right. Powers has to arrange that," Emily agreed.

They drove in silence for a few minutes, then Emily's phone rang. It was Dolores.

"Hi, is everything okay?" she asked.

Instead of Dolores' voice, she heard her daughters, giggling.

"Hi, Mommy!"

"Hi, how was school?" she asked.

"It was good, guess who's here?" Liza asked, giggling again.

"Is it Daddy?"

"No, it's Cousin Angel from Arizona," Juli said.

Emily felt the air go out of her. "Cousin Angel? The one whose house you stayed at?"

"Yeah. She came to visit. Daddy's on his way home and we're going to get Thai food. But guess what? She's going to have a baby!" Liza said, excitedly.

The phone slipped out of Emily's hand; she felt faint. Ryan saw her freeze and grabbed the steering wheel, guiding the car to the shoulder of the highway.

"Mommy? Are you there?" Juli asked.

Emily recovered and grabbed the phone. "Yes, I'm here. But the connection is getting bad. I'll call you later this evening, okay?" Her voice sounded as if she were choking.

"Okay, love you!" the girls said in unison, still giggling.

Emily set the phone down and sat completely still. Her vision blurred. She had no idea what to do with her hands, which felt detached from her body.

"Are you okay, Emily? Are your daughters all right?"

She didn't look at him, keeping her eyes on the road in front of them. "My girls are fine. But you need to drive."

Antonio drove over the speed limit, weaving in between cars on the freeway home from Azusa where he had been testing a new rover.

He replayed the call from Dolores in his head, as if he could change it or make it disappear.

"Anjelica is here at the house... she's with Juli and Liza in the kitchen... you need to come home now..."

He prayed that Emily wouldn't stop at home to see the girls before heading out of town; as he drove, he bartered with God, swearing oaths and promises if He would just keep Emily away until he could get Anjelica out of the house and their lives for good.

He dialed Anjelica's number and she answered, her voice sweet and melodic. "Hi, Toño!"

"What are you doing at our house?" he asked coldly.

"I needed to talk to you about something important and I hadn't heard back from you, so I came by, since I was in town," she explained, as if she were telling him what flavor of coffee she'd ordered that morning.

"This is not okay, Anjelica," he warned her, gripping the steering wheel.

"But I think it is, because here I am!" She laughed, inappropriately.

Anger coursed through him like a jolt of electricity; he wished he could reach through the phone line to shake her.

"I'll be home soon and then we'll leave to go someplace else to discuss this," he said, fighting to remain calm.

"Good. Dolores and I were just talking about a lot of exciting things that are happening right now."

He hung up the phone, wishing with everything in him that he had never crossed paths with her again. That he'd never given in to her flirtations or reciprocated because she made him feel important and special. He hadn't wanted to face it but in therapy he had worked through the uncomfortable truth that part of the attraction to Anjelica was that he felt superior to her.

He made more money than she did, he had a higher level of education. Those things had boosted his ego in a way that now made him feel small and petty. With Anjelica, he would always be the one who was "more," but not with Emily. She was his equal and demanded that he be the best version of himself to keep her. He had failed miserably and all he had accomplished was to ruin the most important things in his life and tonight, he had one last chance to save them.

TWENTY-THREE

Mackenzie was about to sit down to a late lunch of miso soup and Nicoise salad. Kaveri wasn't feeling well with a bad stomachache, so she opted to stay in her room. Gerte could bring her some bone broth later with crackers. Mackenzie was annoyed she hadn't heard back from Zanie with an update, but soon she would be rid of everyone who could cause her problems, including Harry Hubbard. She was just waiting for the right moment to shut him down forever. She took a sip of chilled Pinot Grigio; it was perfect on an autumn day.

Her contact in Tel Aviv had gotten back to her. He admitted that there was ample information on Harry Hubbard and his troublesome proclivities. They were negotiating a price with him to keep them hidden. Mackenzie had offered twice what Hubbard would pay without even knowing the amount. She would let Gideon know when to release the information; it had to be at the precise, correct moment. Harry Hubbard had stepped into a steaming pile of trash and Mackenzie would enjoy watching it burn up and take him down with it.

The guard at the gate called her phone, his voice sounded nervous.

"Ms. Mackenzie, a man named Rawley Jaynes just pushed

through the gate security arm! He asked for you and I was checking his identification when he just blew up and barged his way in! We're on our way up to your house now!"

"Don't worry, Henry. I can manage this situation," she said, hanging up.

In one move, she took a small silver key from her purse and unlocked a safety drawer in the breakfront cabinet. She pulled a nine-millimeter MP Shield from the drawer and slid it into her pocket. Then she heard the front door open. She turned to find Rawley, sweating, with red-rimmed eyes.

"What's going on, Rawley?" she asked calmly, her hand resting on the gun, out of sight in her slim pocket.

"You tell me. Those FBI jerks are still digging into everything. Zanie thinks one of them met with her, undercover, posing as a potential client!" Jaynes barked at her.

Mackenzie was certain he was on a substance of some kind. She stepped toward him, wondering if he could be provoked and she could shoot him in self-defense. That would take care of all her problems with him, but she still needed him to handle a few others.

"Why hasn't Zanie called me back with an update? She said you had someone tailing Emily Ray and Andy Ryan," Mackenzie said.

Jaynes ran his hands over his eyes in agitation. "Zanie isn't going to be calling anyone back, ever. Things got out of hand."

Mackenzie couldn't hold back a smile; Jaynes was tying up the loose ends all on his own.

"Well, we must get rid of anyone who is in the loop, as they say. Anyone who can do us damage and unfortunately, Zanie was one of them. Since you've taken care of her, you should focus on those who remain. Brittney Hoard, for starters," she said, calmly.

"And what about Hubbard?" he demanded.

"I will neutralize Hubbard very soon. That needs to be a strategic strike," Mackenzie said.

Jaynes stepped toward her, menacingly. "Make sure you take

care of it soon. I'll do my part but I don't want any blowback from this. You're the one who started the whole thing with Kaveri!"

Mackenzie pulled the gun from her pocket and fired it once. Jaynes turned pale and froze in place. A single bullet had struck a vintage clock hanging on the wall and cracked the glass face.

"What the hell, Mack?" he asked, afraid to move a muscle.

"You stepped too close to me, Rawley. Don't do that again. You handle your end of things, and I will take care of mine. The FBI agents are for me to deal with."

Jaynes staggered back, wiping his face with his shirt sleeve. "Fine. You just make sure you do it, and the final payment gets deposited into my account."

He lumbered away, leaving his dirty shoe prints on her wheat-colored carpet. She spritzed the room with fresh lemon water and decided in that moment, that if she were ever to be truly free of him, he had to die.

Kaveri jumped when she heard the gunshot. She instinctively crouched down, away from the window, expecting a further barrage of gunfire, but the house was silent. She crept to the door and cracked it open a couple of inches and peered down the hallway. The sound of voices carried from the first floor and then a door slammed shut. She closed and locked the door to her bedroom, leaning against it. The afternoon sun was streaming in her window, a beam of light speckled with small dust particles. She had feigned illness to avoid lunch with Mackenzie; after discovering the microphones in her car and talking with Sierra, she was afraid of her grandmother.

She heard Mackenzie's footsteps approaching and quickly unlocked the door, climbing under her bed covers and slipping on her headphones. When Mackenzie knocked on her door and opened it, Kaveri feigned sleep, feeling her grandmother's eyes on her. She kept her breathing deep and steady, her eyes tightly shut until Mackenzie left. She and Sierra had to speak to the FBI agents as soon as possible. Just to be safe.

Antonio arrived home to find Anjelica in the kitchen with his daughters and Dolores, steely-eyed, folding laundry at the counter.

"Toño!" Anjelica said, rising to greet him with a hug. He stood motionless, his heart pounding with anger.

"Daddy, are we going for Thai food?" Liza asked.

"Cousin Angel said she can come with us," Juli added.

"No, we've had a change of plans, we're having dinner at home and Cousin Angel won't be able to join us," he said. "Why don't we go for a drive, Anjelica?"

She stood and patted the twins on their heads and moved to give Dolores a hug, but the older woman flinched and pulled away. Once outside, they got into his car, and he drove out the gates into the streets of La Cañada.

"What are you doing here?" he demanded.

"You've been ignoring me, so I had no choice but to come and find you," Anjelica said.

"I told you there's nothing between us; it was a mistake. And it's over now."

She laughed softly and looked out the window. "This is a beautiful neighborhood. I'd like to live here," she said, reaching out and patting his hand affectionately. He pushed her touch away.

"Well, you don't and you're not going to," he said.

"Maybe. But there's definitely something still between us. I'm six months pregnant, with your baby," she said, turning toward him while resting her palms on her belly.

Antonio flinched, staring at her in shock, stopping the car abruptly. Behind him, another driver honked in annoyance. Antonio pulled the car to the curb.

"What're you talking about? When?"

"When? You stayed at my house overnight with your daughters. You slept in my bed and we had sex," she said, smoothing her long hair behind her ears, relaxed and seemingly untroubled.

Antonio was silent. He covered his face with his hands, his breathing was labored.

"We barely did it. We stopped halfway through," he said.

"Not halfway enough. Because that's when it happened and I'm not just going to go away and raise your child by myself."

"Angel, we had an understanding..."

She shook her head and laughed, but when she looked at him her eyes were dark and flat with hostility. "We never talked about an 'understanding.' Is it the understanding you had with yourself? That I was like a little shiny pebble that you could pick up and play with and then go back to your real life?"

Antonio's heart pounded so furiously it felt like it might suddenly stop. He had told Emily a half-truth when she'd asked him if he had intercourse with Anjelica. He had gone to Arrowhead to try and fix things with her in person when she found out, and when she asked, he knew that if he told the complete truth, there would be no way back for them. Now, he knew that lie would be the end of everything.

"Anjelica, how do I even know if it's mine?"

She chuckled. "You sound like a podcast bro now, Toño. Playing like you've been trapped? No, you did what you wanted until you got scared and now, there are consequences. If you don't step up, I'll drag you to court for child support and you can explain to your daughters what a deadbeat dad is."

He couldn't even look at her. He thought back to the many times Emily had told him how everything can change in a sliver of a second, a flick of fate. A passing distraction, a lapse in judgment. She dealt with those consequences every day in her work. Now he understood what she meant.

He couldn't even imagine how he would tell his daughters or Dolores. How in time, they would understand what he had done and how it had broken their family. In their eyes he would be that man, for the rest of their lives. Someone who couldn't be trusted.

The type of man they would be cautioned against. He would be his own father with the same story played out again, a continuing cycle of pain and failure.

Anjelica reached out to touch his leg; he pushed her hand away.

"You're upset right now, Toño, but in the end you'll see it was all for the best. You're not happy here, even if you think you are."

He looked at her smile, one that didn't quite reach her eyes, so strangely inappropriate for this moment, caught up in her own delusion. For the first time, he suddenly realized how manipulative and dangerous she was. And he had brought her into the inner circle of his family's life.

TWENTY-FOUR

Sierra had heard the gunshot fired from her mother's house and seen Rawley Jaynes leave in a fit of anger. Whatever unscrupulous scheme Mackenzie had been working on with Jaynes, it was clearly in jeopardy. She knew Kaveri was key to her mother's plans and worried for her safety. The way Mackenzie had put Kaveri on public display as the heir to the family fortune made Sierra certain that it all had to do with money. It always had something to do with money to her family; that was their lifeblood, and no amount was ever enough to satisfy their lust for more.

She dialed the office of the family's longtime law firm, Jackson, Rohner and Gale.

"Hello, this is Sierra Miller Browne, I would like to speak to Mr. Rohner, please."

"Certainly, Ms. Miller Browne. Let me get him," the assistant said with the type of deference the Doucette-Browne name always elicited. A moment later, Jack Rohner came on the line.

"Hello, Sierra! How can I help you?" he asked, affably.

"I'd like a copy of my grandfather's will and trust documents. I know that I'm a trustee and I'd like to review them. You have my email address on file."

Rohner paused and cleared his throat. "I'll have to check on that, Sierra. Your mother is the primary trustee, and you'll need her permission to receive any copies of them."

"Since when? I've looked at them before, I know what's in them." She tried to speak confidently.

"Your mother made the change a few months ago. I can call her and get her approval if you'd like?"

"No, that won't be necessary," Sierra said quickly, before hanging up.

She knew Jack Rohner was likely calling Mackenzie immediately to let her know that Sierra wanted to see the trust documents, which would send her mother into a control-freak meltdown. Sierra called the office of Kittle and Carson, the family's financial planners and received the same response. Mackenzie had shut her out of everything. Sierra would have to find a different way in.

Emily had been quiet since the phone call from home and Ryan didn't want to pry. But he hated seeing her so devastated. She was scrolling through her phone with intense concentration as they drew nearer to the Salton Sea.

"There's not really a town called Frink. It's more like an area adjacent to the Salton Sea. The population of this place is just a few hundred. There's nothing out here," she said, finally. Something inside her had shifted: she had work to do, she couldn't let her personal life derail her job. She'd been so good at compartmentalizing for so long, but she struggled with it now.

"Wasn't it an ill-fated tourist destination? Something went wrong with the water?" Ryan asked.

"Yeah, it became a disaster with really high levels of salt in the runoff from the Imperial Valley and it killed off the fish and birds in the area. I remember it smelling really sour when I'd driven past it."

"How on earth did Jaynes find Kaveri out here?"

"Let's go talk to her former family and friends and see what we learn," Emily said, as they passed a place called Slab City, that appeared to be a collection of graffiti-covered concrete slabs. They pulled into a small trailer park that Stephanie found as Kaveri's address when she was known as Megan Hoard. She had lived with her mother, Brittney, in Space 27. When they arrived, the trailer was locked up with no sign of anyone living there. Through the windows they saw it was empty.

"Maybe her family moved?" Ryan asked.

"It was just her mom, Brittney Hoard. I wonder how long she's been gone?"

"Are you looking for Brittney?"

The voice came from behind them, and they turned to see a skinny blond with frizzy curls, wearing a red tank top and shorts, despite the late-afternoon chill in the desert air. She appeared to be in her late teens or early twenties.

"Can I help you?' the girl asked, more insistent this time.

"Yes, I'm with the FBI. I'm looking for Brittney Hoard, Megan Hoard's mother," Emily said, showing her identification. "This is my partner, Special Agent Andrew Ryan."

"I'm Trina Eagan, Megan's best friend. But she's not here anymore."

"I know, she's been identified as the missing person, Kaveri Miller Browne. We're looking into the case, to discover how she was located and identified. The FBI worked her original abduction years ago and we're following up now that it appears to be solved," Emily lied, hoping to dispel any suspicion Trina might have.

"Oh, okay. That was her mom's place, but she's moved to a manufactured home a few streets over. Yesterday."

"How long have you known Kaveri?" Ryan asked.

Trina laughed, a full-throated easy laugh. "I just can't get my head around calling her Kaveri. She'll always be Megan to me. We've been best friends since before kindergarten."

"You've known her for her entire life, then?" Emily asked.

"Pretty much. My mom says we were inseparable since we were little."

"That's a long time," Ryan said, with a glance to Emily.

"It must've been strange when Rawley Jaynes came around and said she was someone else, I would imagine?" Emily asked.

"Hell, yeah. It was crazy. He came with that little black-haired lady, and they started in about Megan being the lost daughter of this rich lady in Los Angeles and we thought he was nuts!"

"What happened after that?" Ryan asked.

"We blew him off! We thought he was out of pocket. But he sat down one afternoon with Brittney, and they talked for a long time and then, she started telling Megan that she wasn't really her bio mom. That she'd taken her from some cousins of hers who went to Thailand or something. My mom said the whole thing was crazy-ass bullshit. But that black-haired lady took a swab for some DNA from Megan and then said it was a match a few weeks later!"

"Do you miss her?' Ryan asked.

Trina shrugged and squinted at the flat, dry desert that surrounded them.

"Sure. We used to have a lot of fun. We were thinking of maybe going to trade school together. But now..." her voice trailed off, an unfinished thought carried off by the wind.

"Were you, by any chance, the person who called *The World Today* show and told them that Kaveri was a fake?" Emily asked, gently.

Trina kicked at the dirt with her sneakers. "You know about that, huh?"

"If it's true and you've known her since before Kaveri Browne was abducted, then it's pretty important," Emily said.

"I've known Megan forever but that's just 'cause no one remembers being two years old. Brittney came here with Megan when she was a toddler. So, I guess she could've been that girl who was kidnapped."

"Do you have any old photos of you two when you were kids? Maybe before you started school?" Emily asked.

"Yeah, a bunch. I'll find them later, when I get back from the laundromat. I may have to work tonight at the Circle K. You guys gonna be around tomorrow?" she asked.

"Yes. We'll be staying at The Motel by The Sea. We're planning to talk to people who knew Megan and Brittney from the old days," Ryan explained.

"There's not many people here but they all knew Megan. What's your phone number?"

Emily handed her two business cards. "You can reach us at either number."

"I'll text you mine right now," Trina said. "Are you guys married?"

Emily felt the color rush to her cheeks. "No, we're work partners," she blurted.

"Okay, I'll call you tomorrow. You can find Brittney at the Tropicana Home Park over on Rim Rock Road."

"Okay, thanks, Trina!" Ryan said, as she jogged off.

They walked back to the car. Emily searched her phone for the address of Tropicana Home Park.

"Jaynes has some way of finding kids with sketchy background information, like Shirelle Sanders who has no registered birth certificate. I think he matches them with cold case victims. And maybe pays them to go along with the DNA."

"You think that's how Brittney moved into a brand-new house?" Ryan asked.

"Maybe. Amber Hansen and Janelle showed up in a new Highlander. They never had money for a spanking new car before."

"Why do you dislike them so much? It's like you have a bad history with them."

Emily shrugged, trying to play it off. "Sorry. I just got a bad vibe from them. Even when I met Janelle on the Josie Vance case."

Ryan stared out at the vast desert surrounding them. "What kind of asshole goes along with fake DNA when your child has gone missing? Who takes money to say an imposter is real?"

Emily knew her mother, as well as her aunt, would happily take cash to say that Shirelle Sanders was Danica Hansen and that the DNA was a match. She knew they had to have done that for

Jaynes to be parading Shirelle on television. She looked to Ryan, with his youthful outrage and shock at the greed and deceit of average people.

"You're a high-quality man, you know that?" Emily said suddenly.

"No! You make me sound like those guys on podcasts about the male loneliness epidemic!"

"I meant it, seriously. You have such a strong sense of integrity."

"Now I'm the one blushing!" He laughed.

"When did I blush?"

"Back there when Trina asked if we were married."

"I did not! It's hot out here!" Emily protested.

"I saw what I saw, Agent Ray..."

Rawley Jaynes floored the gas pedal of his Porsche, burning rubber in the fast lane of the 10 Freeway. He'd spoken to Norayr who was following the two FBI agents, Emily Ray and Andy Ryan, and they were clearly heading toward Kaveri's old neighborhood.

Zanie had sent him the background information on both of them the day before. At the thought of her lifeless eyes, the bloodstain on the floor, he felt sick to his stomach. Why did she have to make him so angry that he'd grabbed her in that way? He'd picked her up and stashed her in the meat freezer from Best Buy in the garage, the one she convinced him to buy to store steaks and pot roasts. She was so small she fit in easily. He'd deal with Zanie when he got back home.

Right now, Emily Ray and Andy Ryan were arriving at the Salton Sea, in a blue Mercedes GLC. Norayr said they'd spoken to a young woman with frizzy blond hair and Rawley knew it was Trina, Kaveri's best friend. Rawley told him to stay on Emily and Ryan until he got there, then he was free to go. Rawley preferred to take care of his own business. He'd called Brittney and arranged to meet up using the pretext of dropping off some cash. It was amazing what you could accomplish with money.

He believed that most people would sell anything for enough money: their integrity, their self-respect and even people they loved. People like Mackenzie and Jinx had spent their entire lives using money to get what they wanted and expected. But it could only go so far, even for the Doucette-Brownes. Money couldn't save Connor from sticking a needle in his arm. It couldn't make your children love you when you hadn't won their hearts, earned their devotion. Sierra was proof of that.

Despite her bravado, he knew Mackenzie was scared. That's why she wanted everyone who could hurt her eliminated. Brittney Hoard was the most important name on his list. He pulled off the freeway heading toward her new place in the Tropicana Home Park. He texted Norayr for an update on Emily and Ryan.

At salton sea, parked

They were fifteen minutes from where Brittney lived so he had to move quickly. He pulled up to her new place and honked the horn. She stepped out in a pair of cut-off shorts and a 49ers tee-shirt, wearing a big smile. He waved an envelope of money at her.

"Hey, pretty lady! Want to go for a ride?"

She got in and he drove off into the desert, not a moment too soon for Rawley Jaynes.

Emily and Ryan sat in the car, looking at a collection of old trailers, school buses and other makeshift shelters. A group of deeply tanned grizzled men with gray hair moved about the residential installations. The environment appeared hot and hostile.

"This looks like something in *Mad Max*," Ryan whispered.

"And the sun's going to go down soon. This doesn't look like a place we want to be after dark," Emily agreed.

Ten minutes later, they pulled into The Motel by The Sea, a

low-slung, weather-beaten establishment with a chain-link fence and two circular cinderblock arcs to mark the entrance. The rooms were small cabanas grouped around a central patch of dusty ground with a firepit. Beyond the fence line, the open desert went on for miles.

"Somehow the sound of Motel by The Sea gave me a different impression than this," Emily said.

"Me, too. I kind of thought it would be fifties retro, maybe a kidney-shaped pool."

They checked into two adjoining cabanas with thin checkerboard bedspreads and desert-style knick-knacks hung on the wall.

"How about I go pick up dinner and we can eat al fresco by the firepit?" Ryan suggested. "I saw on Yelp that there are some decent-looking restaurants out here. Be back in a few," Ryan said, grabbing the keys and leaving.

Emily sat on the bed, dreading the silence with Ryan gone. She didn't want to think about anything at home; if she did, she might fall into a pit she couldn't pull herself out of. But she couldn't escape the sound of her daughters' voices:

Guess who's here? Cousin Angel...

Daddy's coming home and we're going for Thai food...

She's going to have a baby...

Emily doubted it was a coincidence that Anjelica showed up at their house when she would be away overnight. She wondered what on earth Antonio had been going on about the previous night. He wanted resolution, he wanted an answer from her, to know what her plans were, when he had Anjelica coming over to go out with their kids. Just the idea of them all sitting in a restaurant, eating and being together like a family made her sick.

After so many years together she thought she knew Antonio inside out. But she'd been wrong. Why had he risked their marriage and family for a quick and easy hook-up with an old flame? She would never trust him again. He had pressed her for an answer and now she could give him what he wanted. She knew it was over; there was no way back.

TWENTY-FIVE

Rawley Jaynes drove the deserted roads just outside of Joshua Tree National Park. The landscape was marked with ghostly cholla cactus, standing like an army, floating in the darkness. The desert was still, except for a slight wind that whispered over the moon-like terrain. He was looking for the right place to bury the body of Brittney Hoard, who was lying in his trunk, the life strangled out of her.

Brittney knew way too much about how he worked. She could expose him at any moment if she decided to. It was a big risk to take, getting involved with her, but he had a good sense of people; he knew which ones played by the same type of rules he did. He could always tell who would go along with a con and who would walk away. Most players had too much to lose at some point to become a threat. But for someone like Brittney who had nothing to begin with – and all she had now was a new manufactured home in the middle of nowhere – she could decide she wanted more, as the months and years went on. And with the current threat of the FBI, he couldn't risk that she would say too much.

It had been easy. All he'd had to do was flash that envelope of cash and she willingly came with him. When he drove them into Joshua Tree, she believed him when he said he wanted to see Skull

Rock. She'd followed him across the flat, scrubby dirt babbling about the history of the park and the different plants that grew there. She had been pointing to a rock formation when he slipped his hands around her throat from behind and pinned her body against a boulder with his girth.

It was over more quickly than he'd imagined. He stuck her into his trunk, covered in a beach towel. He remembered a box canyon just outside of the park boundaries and headed there. No one would find her for some time if he hid her well enough. Just a few feet of desert sand and rock would do the trick, so the scavengers would be able to get to her and scatter her remains until they were just a smattering of bleached white bones. She was light enough that he made quick work of it once he found a broken stretch of road in the box canyon. The darkness was complete, the moon half hidden by a cloud.

He put her in the ground, covered with dried cactus branches and rocks. He heard an eerie cry, like a baby, and hurried back to his car. Coyotes didn't make that sound, but mountain lions did, while luring prey out into the killing zone. He knew he wasn't the apex predator in this fierce, pitiless landscape. He got into his car and made a quick U-turn, heading back toward Salton City to finish up his work.

It was dark when Ryan returned with two takeout bags of dinner.

"The sun goes down so quickly out here, it's kind of spooky! I found a gourmet burger place and they had a veggie burger so I made the executive decision that you might prefer that one."

"Thanks, you know me well," Emily said. He was so thoughtful.

He opened another grocery store bag and set a cold six pack of Cut Water Margaritas on the dresser.

"And these. I don't know, I thought we might like them," he said with a shy grin.

"I don't usually drink when I'm working but I think this is a good day to make an exception," Emily agreed.

They sat at the firepit, the only guests. With no streetlights, the stars spread out like a painting with their shimmering pinpoints of light. Emily and Ryan each drank a canned margarita and leaned back in their respective chairs, watching for shooting stars.

"There's one!" Ryan said, pointing to a streak of silver light that traversed the heavens.

Emily felt the effects of the margarita; she never drank much and rarely any hard liquor. But it tasted much better than she expected and the slight buzz felt good. They sat in silence for several minutes.

"Do you want to talk about what happened on your phone call earlier or not?" Ryan asked, finally.

Emily took another sip of her drink, weighing whether she should tell Ryan the whole ugly truth. He'd never been anything less than loyal and kind to her, even under the stress of work and in the risky take-down of James Tibbs. She rested the can on the arm of her chair, leaned her head back, closed her eyes and said, "Last night my husband was all about wanting to know what's going on with us, he wants to fix it, etc. And then my daughters, who don't know anything about what happened, called today to tell me that the woman he had a fling with is at our house. And she's going to have a baby!"

Ryan let out a long exhale and said, "That's bad, like really bad."

"Right? I doubt she just showed up. He knew I'd be gone and the whole thing is just... messed up," she said quietly, feeling the effects of the liquor. She stared out into the darkness that surrounded them, then hung her head in defeat.

"That's not even something you get over; that's part of your life forever."

"Yeah. And forever is a very long time."

Emily reached for a second can of Cut Water, then continued.

"It's like... you think you've made something, this life, this family and then you realize, you don't have anything. It never mattered that much to him. Suddenly it's all just like... nothing..." her voice faltered.

Ryan opened another can, shaking his head, letting out a heavy sigh. "Who would do that? I mean, as a man, with a family? I just don't get it."

"What about you?" Emily asked. "How're you doing with the broken engagement?"

Ryan smiled sadly. "It's miserable. But I've had a broken engagement before, not that it really helps."

"Really? What was his name?" Emily asked, leaning in.

"It was a woman and her name was Catherine," he replied.

"A woman? I thought you were..."

Ryan cut her off. "Gay? Well, sexuality is... different for everyone, I guess. Erik was the first man I ever had a relationship with. I'd had an interest and urges before that. I'd had some flings but never a full-blown relationship."

"So, what was Catherine like?" Emily asked, the drink had gone to her head and she felt woozy.

"She was great. Smart, funny, kind, really pretty. She's a doctor now. I was in love with her. I'd always dated women; I was a jock in school." He took another sip of his drink, staring at the flickering flames of the fire. "But I also had... an attraction to men. I wasn't tortured about it; it was... just part of the general landscape of my love life. I think, for me, it's really about the person, you know? What qualities does this individual person have that I'm attracted to?"

"That's good. Better than objectifying people based on sex, which is so common," Emily said, feeling completely relaxed for the first time in a long while.

Ryan took a long swig from his drink, his head felt light but nice, like he was floating.

"I guess for some people it's clear cut. They are completely straight or gay. We have this polarity in society. But for me, it's more... fluid. And that goes in both directions," he said with an embarrassed laugh.

Emily asked, "How'd you and Catherine break up?"

"We were engaged, but I knew I still had an attraction to men. I'd always felt it, and I knew I had to tell her before we got married. It would've been wrong to not let her know. Not that I would've done anything about it once we were married and had taken vows. But she said she couldn't really deal with that, so we broke up. I met Erik a couple of years later and felt like maybe that was it."

"Wow. Do you think you'd ever go back to dating women?" Emily asked.

"Maybe. I'm not thinking about all of that right now," Ryan replied, handing her another can of Cut Water.

"I shouldn't drink this," Emily said, taking the can.

"I shouldn't either," Ryan said, popping his open.

They sat in silence, staring up at the sky for a long time. The fire died down to a faint flickering of flames, dancing as it burnt out. A car drove down the dusty road to the motel and started to turn in but then zigged back onto the road and disappeared.

"We should go in and get some sleep. We've got a lot to do tomorrow," Emily said.

"Agreed."

Ryan tossed the empty cans into a trash and covered the firepit to extinguish the remaining embers. When they arrived at the cabanas, Emily stepped into her room, Ryan hung in the doorway.

"Thanks for picking up dinner. It was fun to unwind," Emily said.

"I know. It's nice to just... hang out. These cases can be so... unrelenting."

They stared at each other for a beat, then suddenly Ryan leaned forward, slipped his arm around her waist and kissed her. Emily felt her body freeze; she stood stock-still. Ryan stepped back awkwardly.

"I'm sorry. I shouldn't have done that. It's the alcohol," he apologized.

"No, you shouldn't have," she said huskily, her eyes still closed. "But you should... do it again... just to be sure."

"I should?" he asked, his voice sounded like a dog's squeaky toy.

"Just to be sure that... we shouldn't do this," she said, feeling the full effects of the alcohol. Her thoughts bounced from Ryan's dark eyes to Antonio's hollow attempts at reconciliation. She didn't want to think about it, to try to figure out how she felt and what she wanted. She didn't want to think about anything. Ryan kissed her again; this time she felt her knees go wobbly beneath her.

"I think we are doing this," he said, stepping in to her and gently backing her up against the wall, kicking the door shut behind him with one swift move.

"But we're both upset about other people," Emily said, searching half-heartedly for a reason as she leaned in and kissed him, sliding her tongue into his mouth and hearing him let out a small gasp of surprise.

He dropped his hands to the waistband of her slacks and pulled her up against him.

"Oh my. I guess you are attracted to women," she said quietly.

He rested his forehead against hers and whispered, "Yes, I am."

TWENTY-SIX

Trina looked at the clock over the door of the Circle K. It was almost eleven o'clock. The street outside was deserted. Beyond the halo of light thrown by the streetlamps, the desert dissolved into total darkness. She closed the blinds at the front window. The owner, Denise McIntyre, insisted that she stay open even when there was no business in town after nine.

Just that afternoon, Trina had asked to close early, given the season and the cold weather that descended over the desert at night and kept people indoors. Denise had stood at the counter, her thinning blond hair and fleshy face etched into a perpetual frown, shaking her head.

"No way, Trina. We need to get those people driving up to Joshua Tree."

"But who's making that drive at night? It's two hours!" Trina complained, but Denise wouldn't have it.

"There's lots of people who'd be happy to take this job, girlie," Denise threatened.

Trina bit back her frustration; there weren't even a lot of people in the entire town and no one else wanted to sit in a cold convenience store selling Takis and energy drinks at night. But she needed the job, so she stayed quiet as Denise left and got into her beat-up turquoise Grand Cherokee and drove off.

Trina's last customer had been over two hours ago, a dark-haired guy with a short beard and an accent. He'd been polite and paid in cash, buying a can of Coke and some off-brand Twinkies. Then he'd left, driving his black SUV onto the highway.

She'd waited until a quarter to eleven to start closing and counted the meager money that was taken in and put it in the cash bag in the small safe. She wiped down the counters and emptied the coffee machines, refilling the water for the next morning and ran a damp mop over the dusty floor and closed the blinds. At eleven, she grabbed her bag and stepped out into the night, turning to close and lock the door behind her.

She didn't see someone step up and put a gloved hand over her mouth, kicking her legs out from under her before shoving her into the open door of a black Porsche.

It was past midnight when Emily woke and turned to see Ryan, fast asleep, half covered by the thin sheet. Her head hurt and her mouth felt like a pile of cotton balls. She tiptoed to the bathroom and took a long drink from the faucet, slipping into the pajamas she had intended to wear to bed. She pulled her hair back into a scrunchie and took stock of what had happened that evening.

She pulled the curtain back just a few inches, so the outdoor light fell across Ryan's sleeping body. He was so handsome and his physique, freed from a business suit and dress shirt, was like a sculpture. He was a full ten years younger than she was and she couldn't quite believe that he was right there, under the covers.

She bit back a guilty smile, knowing she should feel dreadful but not quite finding her way there. She thought of Antonio who had spent days in Arizona courting Anjelica, while Dolores watched and grew more upset. Of him taking their daughters for a sleepover, intending to stay over himself in Anjelica's bedroom, the place they had conceived the baby that was the final straw that destroyed her marriage.

She and Ryan had simply had too many margaritas under the desert moon and commiserated about their mutual heartbreak, leading them to an explosive and sudden encounter. She had never been with anyone but her husband.

Being with Andy Ryan had been an epiphany. It was completely different: his energy, his touch, his rhythm. Part of her enjoyed that she had repaid her husband's betrayal in kind, even if it was a petty sentiment. They were separated and hadn't slept in the same room or had sex for months. This wasn't the same as what he did with Anjelica. This was altogether different.

She slipped outside into the cool night air and checked her phone. She had missed several calls from Antonio but her anger at him was still too raw. If it had been about her daughters, Dolores would have called. She sat in a folding chair, pulling her flannel pajamas close around her, waiting for her eyes to adjust to the dark. A black Porsche cruised slowly down the dirt road with its headlights off and pulled into the parking area of the motel. Emily instinctively stepped back inside the room and watched the car from the window. She had glimpsed the same car earlier.

Something was off; no one would drive on a pitch-black desert road with no headlights, at one o'clock in the morning. A man stepped out and as he went into one of the cabanas, he passed under the outside light, and she gasped. It was Rawley Jaynes. Emily heard Ryan stir and he stepped over to join her at the window, clad in his PJ bottoms.

"What're you looking at?" he whispered.

"That car, the black Porsche that cruised by earlier, it's Rawley Jaynes."

"We must be doing something that he wants to interfere with," he said, reaching for his holster and unlocking his gun. Emily did the same and zoomed in on the license plate with her phone, snapping several photos. Then they sat in the dark at the window and waited.

. . .

Senator Harry Hubbard paced in his Beverly Hills hotel room, unable to sleep. Even two double Scotches hadn't helped him drift off. Every minute that went by brought him that much closer to total ruin. Uriel, the blackmailer, could destroy him in one move, wipe out his long legacy. And if Uriel's information got out, there would be more to follow. Escorts and partygoers he had met over the years on the circuit of social events that filled his calendar, populated by his colleagues and co-workers who shared his proclivities. They would come forward with stories too lurid for his God-fearing southern Christian constituents to handle or forgive. He wished he could call up those FBI agents and squeeze the information out of them but now that he was in town, he'd be able to turn up the pressure.

Was Kaveri Browne really who they said she was? It was all too convenient, in his opinion. Whoever thought she would show up again, alive and well? He assumed she'd been kidnapped and murdered by some lunatic and they'd be lucky if they found remnants of her remains. He wanted an answer, so he knew what to expect, to prepare for it. He'd pay a visit to old Jinx Doucette-Browne in person. To get answers. He called SAC John Powers to leave a message, even if it was the middle of the night. He needed to be appeased, while he could still make people pay for their failures against him.

TWENTY-SEVEN

Emily awoke early and took a quick shower, turning the faucet to the cold setting for a couple of minutes before stepping out. Her head pounded as a hangover settled in, with no intention of leaving. The cold water helped but she needed a big breakfast with a carbohydrate boost. A protein bar and hotel black coffee would not cut it.

Ryan had gone back to his own room after they abandoned surveillance on Rawley Jaynes to catch a couple of hours of sleep. Neither of them had the courage to face waking up next to each other in the same bed. She planned to dial Trina at nine to arrange a meeting and see what photos and other evidence she had of Kaveri as a baby.

Half an hour later, she was checking them out of the motel as Ryan emerged, freshly showered, looking like a college boy in his casual tee-shirt and jeans. He smiled at her and caught himself as he reached for her waist in a gesture of familiarity.

"Jaynes is gone," she said, gesturing to the parking lot.

"We'll find him. How's your head?" he asked.

"It feels like it's been in the dryer all night. How about you?"

"Same. Should we catch breakfast first?"

"Yeah, I looked up a couple of places online. I need strong coffee and something heavy, like eggs and pancakes," Emily said.

They walked to the dusty parking lot, their car was the only one parked. The morning light in the desert was stark and brilliant.

"Jaynes must've left pretty early," Ryan said.

Emily went inside to check with the clerk to see if they had a name for the driver of the Porsche.

The clerk said, "Sure. He came in last night, a few hours after you two arrived. His name is Baron Lee. He left real early."

As they drove to the Hungry Bear Family Restaurant, Ryan said, "So, do we just pretend last night didn't happen and forget about it? I don't want to be presumptuous, I know you don't drink often, and you were intoxicated. And you're upset with your husband."

Emily nodded and said, "Let's definitely pretend it never happened because we're working together and we're both going through relationship stuff. But we shouldn't forget about it."

"Okay, why not?" Ryan asked shyly.

Emily looked out the window, self-consciously. "Because it was... too incredible to forget."

Ryan kept his eyes on the road as a smile spread across his face and said, "It's good to be a grown-up, isn't it?"

They ate a quick breakfast and hurried to Trina's trailer; she hadn't been answering Emily's calls. As they drove into the trailer park, they saw a large fire truck and two police cars parked outside the trailer where Trina lived with her mother, who was seated outside on a plastic folding chair. Behind her the trailer was a charred heap of metal and wood.

When Emily and Ryan approached, the woman asked, "Are you the FBI people? Trina said you talked to her yesterday, about Kaveri. She had gotten some photos together, but they're gone now," she said weakly, gesturing to the ruin of her trailer. "I don't got no insurance either."

"Is Trina here?" Emily asked, worried.

"No, she didn't come home last night. I've been calling and calling her but there's no answer."

At this point a local police office stepped in and asked to see their identification, then he said, "There's no sign of her at the Circle K either. The place was in perfect condition and no sign of foul play."

"Any security footage?" Ryan asked.

"The cameras are just for show. Her car is also still there."

Emily leaned into Ryan and said quietly, "I think this has to do with us speaking to her. I'm calling Powers now; this has turned into something way more than a personal favor for Hubbard. We need subpoenas, financials, all of it."

While Ryan spoke with Trina's mother, Emily dialed SAC Powers' office in Los Angeles. His assistant put her through right away.

"Hello, Emily. How's it going?" Powers asked.

"Not good, sir. Since we've started this, one person is dead, and one is missing. I think there is something much bigger at play here."

"Are those events directly related to Kaveri Miller Browne?"

"Mackenzie Browne won't deal with us; she has no reason to. We have no charges or legitimate suspicion of a crime. But we have two people who've been impacted by us asking these questions. One of them died unexpectedly in her assisted living facility and the other one is missing, after agreeing to meet with us today to give us information about Kaveri Browne. We need real authority to subpoena bank and phone records, we need..."

Powers interrupted her, "Someone in an assisted living facility could have died for any reason. Getting those subpoenas will not be possible, Emily. This request came through a personal channel and if we begin with subpoenas and the rest, it will have to come to light. Isn't it possible that these two situations you've described are simply a coincidence?"

Emily took a deep breath to control her anger. "I don't think so, sir. These inquiries seem to have put people in danger, and we have a responsibility to investigate properly."

"Let me make some phone calls and get back to you. In the meantime, under no circumstances are you or Ryan to get involved in these incidents. They are not in our jurisdiction, and the FBI plays no official role in either case," Powers said, before hanging up.

Emily wanted to throw the phone across the concrete in frustration. She returned to the local cops outside Trina's trailer and pulled up the photos of the black Porsche and of Rawley Jaynes.

"We're conducting a possible fraud investigation, and we were supposed to speak with Trina Eagan this morning. It involves this individual, and we believe he followed us out here. He stayed at The Motel by The Sea and came back last night very late, with the headlights off," she explained.

The cop took a screenshot of the license plate.

"He's probably heading back toward the L.A. area or the inland Empire. He might have something to do with Trina Eagan's disappearance," Ryan said.

As they walked back to the car, Emily said, "I don't want you breaking any rules on this, Andy. Powers doesn't want us involved in this case but there's no way I'm going to let these small-town cops handle this if we can steer them in a better direction. You're new at the FBI. I never should've gotten you into this so let me take the fall if there are any repercussions, okay?"

Ryan looked at her like she'd lost her mind. "Like that's going to happen. We're partners in this, Em. If there's fallout from it, I'm standing right beside you."

They drove to Brittney's home and saw that it was still dark and unoccupied. This time, her car was in the driveway. They knocked but got no answer. As they walked the perimeter of the house, an elderly neighbor stepped out. She was a tiny, gray-haired woman with large glasses.

"Can I help you?" she asked warily.

"We're looking for Brittney Hoard. She moved in a couple of days ago," Ryan said.

"Oh, yes. She left with that fellow in the sports car. Yesterday, in the afternoon."

"Do you remember what he looked like?" Emily asked, pulling up a photo of Rawley Jaynes. "Is this him?"

The woman looked closely at the photo. "It might be. But I know the car was a Porsche. My son has one just like it."

Emily handed her a business card. "If she returns could you ask her to call me?"

As they walked to the car, Ryan said, "I'm calling Officer Cortez to let him know. Now we have two missing people in under twenty-four hours. Something is spinning out of control!"

Sierra pushed the door to her grandfather's room open and stepped in. Sozi had gone to get her lunch from the main kitchen and Gerte was busy directing the window cleaners outside. The drapes in Jinx's room were half drawn and despite the humidifier and air fresheners, it smelled like death. Jinx had no idea who anyone was most of the time, so she didn't bother trying to wake him from his nap. She'd already checked his office, which just collected dust now that he was bedridden. In her childhood, he had sat at his ornate desk like a king, presiding over mergers and takeovers, forced bankruptcies and hedge funds. Breaking lives and building capital.

Now, he was like a corpse, skin and bones stretched thin over his withering body. She wondered what drove him to cling to life when it was such a battle. No doubt he had been like most powerful men, chasing immortality like a hungry leopard. If he had enough buildings and hospitals with his family name on them or museum wings filled with his donations, he would live forever and avoid the dark, anonymous pit of death. Her mother was the same way, both of them driven to fill an empty void that they carried inside. Sierra knew her grandfather was old school and kept paper copies of all his important documents. The family trust documents could be hidden in a drawer or under a box, those were eccentricities Jinx was known for.

She had to get those documents to see if anything they

contained was tied to Kaveri. If the girl was just a pawn in Mackenzie's plan, then Kaveri would be discarded once she was no longer necessary and she might be in danger that Sierra needed to protect her from. If that were the case, they also needed to reach out to Emily Ray and Andy Ryan immediately for help. She looked in closets and under furniture, in drawers and behind books. She found nothing. Her grandfather awoke with a start and raised a bony finger at her.

"Kaveri? Is... that you?" he rasped.

Sierra went to his bed. "No, it's Sierra. Your granddaughter. Mackenzie's daughter."

His cloudy eyes were confused then he shook his head.

"Be careful... of... your mother..." he said, before sputtering phlegm from the effort of speaking.

For the first time in her life, Sierra saw fear in the old man's eyes.

TWENTY-EIGHT

Harry Hubbard's entourage arrived at the entrance to the Doucette-Browne compound unannounced. He had an early meeting with donors and felt it would be better not to give Mackenzie an opportunity to avoid him easily. He didn't care about seeing her; he needed to meet with Jinx to see exactly how close to death he was; everything hung on that occurrence.

When the guard at the security kiosk buzzed him in, Hubbard's driver pulled onto the estate that Hubbard had visited so many times in his career. As they drove up toward the big house, Hubbard recalled fondly the parties and weekends of unabashed debauchery they had enjoyed. Jinx always paid for the best entertainment, the prettiest boys and girls, the best food and liquor.

As he stepped out of the car, Mackenzie walked out to meet him, wearing a flat smile when she saw Hubbard's assistant and advance team getting out of the other car in his entourage. A photographer was at the ready to capture a photo of them together with the palatial mansion behind them.

"Mackenzie, my dear!" Hubbard said, greeting her.

"Senator, we had no idea you were coming. To what do we owe the pleasure?" she asked. The photographer snapped away.

"Just in town for the usual political hat-in-hand with the donors. I was hoping to have a chance to see your dear father?"

"Let me check with his attendant. His health is very poor these days. Why don't you go in and have my staff serve you something to drink?" Mackenzie offered, guiding him toward the main door of the house.

She handed him off to her maid and headed for her father's wing of the house. She found Jinx, sitting up in bed, his eyes bleary, watching an old episode of *Barnaby Jones*. Sozi was in the bathroom, organizing his medication.

"Daddy, your old friend Harry Hubbard is here to see you. Are you up for that?" Mackenzie asked.

Jinx looked at her blankly, then nodded. He moved his lips to speak but he could not form words. He had declined so much in recent days. Mackenzie smiled, sure that her father had no idea what she had said or who was visiting him. Harry Hubbard would find himself face to face with a withered, empty shell of her formidable father, unable to communicate his wants or needs. She smiled to herself in satisfaction. It was what they both deserved.

A few minutes later, Hubbard entered the room, while Mackenzie stood in the doorway. Sozi sat on the couch, keeping a watchful eye on the old man.

"Well, hey there, Jinx old man!" Hubbard said, enthusiastically.

Jinx just nodded in his direction, his fingers clutching at his pajamas. Hubbard sat on the edge of the bed, staring into Jinx's cloudy eyes, realizing that his hope of extracting some kind of financial guarantee out of Jinx was ill-founded. The business of Kaveri being returned had thrown a wrench into his plans when he could not afford it and he'd figured he might get some other type of arrangement set up. But Jinx was well past the ability to reason or make any plans at all.

As if she could read his mind, Mackenzie said, "His doctors deemed him mentally incompetent over eight months ago. Anything he says or signs is invalid."

Hubbard nodded at her, his face a mask of polite dismay. He stood to go; Jinx did not notice.

"Well, it was nice to see him, one last time," Hubbard said, taking Mackenzie's hand, which she withdrew from his grasp.

"Nice to see you, too, Senator."

"Give my best to Kaveri and Sierra."

"I will. They're out shopping today."

As Hubbard headed down the hallway he saw Gerte Brose coming up the stairs, carrying a pile of freshly laundered towels.

He looked at her in surprise and said, "Is that you, Gerte? Are you still with the old man even after all this time?"

Gerte looked at him, her face impassive as she nodded. She walked past him, and he leaned over, taking her arm and whispered, *"Willst du eine gute Zeit haben?"*

Rawley was still in the flatlands of the Mojave when he saw two police cars riding his tail, with their lights flashing. In a moment of panic, he considered cutting across the lanes of the freeway and trying to escape them across the desert, but it was futile. He hoped it was a simple traffic violation, perhaps one of his taillights had broken. He pulled over, acutely aware of the dirty, blood-stained clothing in his duffel bag. His tires were covered with dust and desert debris. He had clearly driven off-road recently. He chastised himself for not driving through a gas station car wash before he left Salton City.

An officer walked up and tapped on his window, his eyes hidden behind large sunglasses.

"May I see your license and registration, sir?"

Rawley retrieved both with a grin. "Here they are, officer. I'm a retired cop, a homicide detective out of L.A. Part of the thin blue line brotherhood!"

The officer nodded as he looked over Jaynes' documents then went to the cruiser to make a radio call. Rawley fidgeted, watching the two cops from the second cruiser as they walked around his car, checking out the dirt and debris on his tires.

The officer returned and said, "Would you step out of the car please, Mr. Jaynes? We need to take you in for questioning in two missing persons cases."

Jaynes stepped out into the mid-morning heat of the desert, the wind whipping the dirt across the highway. He knew he was screwed. It was time to call in favors.

Emily and Ryan got word of Jaynes being picked up as they were getting close to Riverside. Back in Salton City, the police had seen Jaynes' car on various security cameras around town, and they were retracing the routes he drove in hopes of finding some sign of Trina or Brittney.

"What do you think the chances are of getting new DNA on Danica and Kaveri?" Ryan asked.

"On Kaveri, no chance. Mackenzie will never agree to it. With Danica it might be easier. I know a good DNA person at Stemma Lab in Orange County. Elsbeth Winter. I used her for the Josie Vance case."

"If we can expose that there is an issue with any DNA run by Rawley Jaynes, then all of it becomes suspect and we might get a clear answer on Kaveri that way. Or at least another test if he's tampered with it," Ryan suggested.

Emily nodded, pensive. Then she said, "I'm beginning to wonder why we're doing any of this. If Kaveri is a fraud, who does it hurt? Is anyone going to suffer because of it?"

"What about Danica? If she's a fake, the real woman could be out there somewhere, hoping to be found and the investigation would be closed if they say she's been located."

Emily paused. "What if she doesn't want to be found?"

Before Ryan could answer, her phone rang. It was Stephanie Leedom.

"What's up, Steph? We're driving back, you're on speaker."

"I just found something interesting. The woman who works with Rawley Jaynes, Zanie Lichtman. She has a sister who works in the public records office for the state, up in Sacramento. She's been there for years. She has access to all state records. Her name is Melanie Lichtman."

"As in birth and death certificates?" Ryan asked.

"Yes, all of it. And guess what? Megan Hoard's birth was not registered until she was three years old."

"Thanks, Steph. This is great," Emily said, hanging up.

"So, she could be Kaveri Browne and Brittney took custody of her as a toddler, just like Mackenzie says," Emily said.

"Or it could be like you said, he's using Melanie to get access to information that fits his needs."

Emily fell quiet, with the unsettling realization that if Kaveri Browne were really Megan Hoard, they had a lot in common. Emily knew what it was to come from a family and place that offered her no options. She knew what it was to be in and out of foster care and the stigma that came with it. She had changed placements where they gave her a black trash bag to pack her belongings, as if she had no greater value than garbage.

Seeing firsthand the desolation of Frink and Salton City, she knew that life as Kaveri Browne would give Megan the chances that life had placed beyond her reach. Just as it had for her when she took on Emily's identity and suddenly had a parent who loved her, financial security and a stable support system. Those things made college possible and her career with the FBI as well as her marriage and parenthood where she could give her daughters the same advantages. Becoming Emily Ray had given her a full and productive life.

Whatever it was that Harry Hubbard wanted from their unofficial investigation could not be as valuable as the chance now given to Megan, who may well have known nothing of the deals made that treated her life like a playing card in a betting game. But they had come this far, and she knew Powers would push them to get proof that Jaynes was committing fraud, if it helped his old friend and crony. Now she and Ryan were pawns in a bigger game that she wanted no part of.

Gerte hurried to her room, after putting the towels into the big linen closet. She closed the door and leaned against it, blocking it with her body. She was breathing heavily, sweating. Seeing Harry Hubbard's face, so close to hers, feeling his breath on her neck, had triggered a memory she'd buried, of another night decades ago when she had leaned against the same door to block it. She shut her eyes and slid down to the floor, folding in over herself.

Mr. Jinx had bought her a closet full of casual clothes and uniforms but for this evening, he had asked her to wear the pale green party dress he had brought home that afternoon... she'd put her blond hair in braids as he'd requested. She walked down the big staircase where there was music playing and food being served on small plates being passed around...

Someone handed her a fizzy drink, it tasted like melons and tickled her nose... then Mr. Jinx was there, so handsome in his dark suit, taking her hand, leading her down the long hallway toward the east wing of the house... her head felt light and she stumbled on the Persian carpet, the toe of her Mary-Jane shoe catching on the thick pile...

"You look so pretty tonight, Gerte, a proper little fraulein," he said, running his smooth hand over her blond braids...

The door opened and he led her into the big library room, filled with bookcases and rugs, a fire was burning in the hearth... it looked like a scene from the Brothers Grimm fairy tales... she smiled and looked at all the faces smiling back at her... then she realized they were all men... the lady guests were in a different part of the house... she turned but Mr. Jinx caught her arm and she saw that the door was closed...

She felt faint... unsteady, but Mr. Jinx put a strong arm around her waist... then his hand was under her dress, pushing and pulling

*at her white tights... she felt them tear and his hand, insistent...
cold... prodding at her flesh...*

*"No, stop, Mr. Jinx..." she tried to cry out, but her voice was
thick...*

*... then so many hands, so many faces right next to hers... their
breath smelled of whiskey and cigarettes... hands, pulling at her
arms... her legs... pushing her down onto the black leather sofa... the
fire was roaring... the room was so hot...*

*Then the pale eyes of Harry Hubbard... so close to hers... his
voice in her ear.*

Willst du eine gute Zeit haben?

Do you want to have a good time?

The laughter... the others joining in...

Willst du eine gute Zeit haben?

Then the pain began...

Gerte sat against the door, curled up, quiet sobs racking her
body. She had buried the memory, deep in a mental lockbox.
There was no way to process it at the time. She was a teenager,
newly arrived, lucky to have a job in America in a fine house. She
had good food to eat each day, more than her parents could give her
in the old country. There was always heat in the big house, not like
the cold two-room flat she had shared with her siblings and parents
in the bitter Bavarian winters.

She wore well-made clothes of real wool and cotton. There was
a garden full of fresh fruit and the California sun, no snow or sleet,
no icy roads to skin her knees on. Every day was warm and beautiful. She was the lucky one, she couldn't return to her family as a
failure, having left service for Mr. Jinx, no matter what happened.
She had to endure.

And he held her passport in a locked safe in his office. After
that night, she learned from the other servants that this was part of
living in the big house. All the young girls and boys were required
to be present at Mr. Jinx's parties and attend to his guests in the
library. Where no one could hear you scream.

After that, she had hidden every time there was a party, either in the deep pantry in the kitchens or out in the chicken coop. When she returned one night, with chicken excrement on her shoes and feathers in her hair, Mr. Jinx was waiting for her.

"Look at you! Coming back in like the little disgusting piglet that you are! You smell of shit and chicken feed!" he said, his eyes glazed from alcohol, his tie undone.

She'd been too afraid to respond and kept her eyes down. He walked around her, as if he were at a livestock auction.

"You don't want to be part of my little entertainments any longer, Gerte? You think you're too good for us, little Bavarian peasant. That's fine. You're like a stupid farm animal. You look like a milk maid with those wide hips and thighs, not like a little girl," he said, his words slurred as he pushed her away.

After that, he gave her the hardest jobs to do in the house on party days, but he never made her attend again. She could hide in her locked bedroom, trying to ignore that other young staffers had to attend to his guests. Ilse. Johan. Louise.

Gerte stood up, her legs were stiff from crouching for so long. She moved to the mirror and saw her reflection. The lines on her face, and her severe gray haircut gave her the look of a prison matron. A sturdy body clad in the same style uniform she had worn for fifty years. Thick legs and arms, a torso like a fallen log but the extra weight had helped her stay safe. Better to be heavy and undesirable than a beautiful, lithe party favor.

She'd never been on a dinner date or to the county fair. Never shopped in the fine stores or been to the salon where they served you cocktails or fancy coffee. Never walked in leisure down a wide boulevard, looking in shop windows. She was too afraid of everything and everyone after that terrifying night.

Back then, she was young and powerless, in an unfamiliar country. Now Jinx Doucette-Browne was the one who was fragile and powerless, unable to move, barely able to speak. She had never thought of revenge. Until now.

TWENTY-NINE

Mackenzie received the call from Rawley who was being held by the police in Coachella Valley, and she almost laughed at the absurdity of it. She had never even heard of Coachella Valley. She had arranged for her lawyer to drive out and meet with him to assure him he was not alone. She had to keep him quiet for the time being until she could make further plans for him. He affirmed that he had dealt with both Brittney Hoard and Kaveri's childhood friend, Trina Eagan, who talked too much. With them gone, and Zanie dead, Jaynes was the only one who could drag her down. Melanie Lichtman had too much to lose to ever come clean about her role.

Mackenzie liked doing business that way, so everyone had more to lose than she did. And didn't have an endless money stream to pay lawyers for court cases that could drag on for years. The lawyer, Bob Lackey, would soothe Rawley's nerves and get him under control, creating the illusion that Mackenzie had his back, never realizing that the only thing she had on his back was a target.

. . .

Melanie Lichtman called her sister, Zanie, from the back seat of her Uber. No answer again. She'd been trying for the past day but gotten no response. She'd received a call from Mackenzie Miller Browne to let her know that Rawley had been detained for questioning in the disappearances of two women related to Kaveri's return. The phone call was as much of a warning as it was an update on her sister's boyfriend. Mackenzie said that two FBI agents were looking into Kaveri at the request of a senator.

When Melanie heard "FBI" and "Senator" she knew that something big was about to hit and she was not going to be around to get leveled by it. She wished she had never gotten involved in Zanie's plan, but she wanted her sister to finally have some real financial stability after a lifetime of running one low-level con after another. Rawley was a bottom-feeder, but he'd been a cop and a detective. He had credibility and when they came up with the Home at Last scheme, she agreed to help.

She knew that the kids who had disappeared years ago were never going to be found. Those things only happened in Lifetime movies. Kids like Kaveri Miller Browne were not coming home. Neither was Danica Hansen. And everyone likes a happy ending, so if she could help provide one, she had no problem with it. It gave Zanie a chance to have a real life, maybe even get married to Rawley and have a family of her own.

She had access to all the birth certificates in the state. She could easily search for hospital and home births, the kids who didn't get properly registered immediately. The kids whose paperwork had wiggle room that Rawley and Zanie could use and fill in the blanks with their own story. And Zanie was good at figuring out who could be bought off for a nice sum of cash. She could read criminality or desperation in someone like a bomb-sniffing dog. It was teamwork between sisters for the common good, that was how Melanie liked to see it.

Her flight to Nicaragua was departing LAX in an hour and a half. She kept enough cash on hand at home to be able to float under the radar for as long as she needed to. Their father, Leo, had taught them that. She was headed to a beach oasis so far off the beaten path, she had to take two buses to get there. A shiver of worry ran up her spine, as she thought of Zanie. It wasn't like her to not return calls, but Zanie could take care of herself.

Ryan pulled the car into the parking lot of Ontario Airport; Emily had made flight reservations en route for them to fly to Las Vegas and then make the hour-and-a-half drive to Baker to meet with the Sanders family and Danica Hansen.

Emily wished they didn't have to go through the charade of testing Danica's DNA, but she had to follow the protocols since she couldn't admit the truth. Now she had to face the encounter she had been dreading, and sit across from the woman claiming the identity that she had left behind. Someone else had claimed it, an imposter, just like she was. It felt surreal, like a bad drug trip that she couldn't escape.

It was late afternoon when they checked in at the airline gate. With luck, they might be home by midnight. Emily had ignored several calls from Antonio but when she saw his number come up again, she walked away to take the call.

"Em? Is everything okay?" he asked gently.

"Yes, we've just been traveling to do interviews for this investigation."

"When will you be home?"

"Late tonight. I'll call the girls before bedtime to talk to them."

"Okay, there's some stuff we need to talk about," he said. She could hear the hesitancy in his voice.

She didn't respond for a beat, trying to find the right words to say.

"I know, okay?" she said sharply.

"You know what?" he asked.

"About Anjelica showing up at our house and that she's pregnant."

Now he was silent, it seemed that he had stopped breathing.

"Did Dolores talk to you?" he asked, finally.

"No, the girls called me to say that Cousin Angel was at the house and guess what? She's having a baby!" Emily said, a hollow laugh escaping her throat.

"The girls spoke to you? They never mentioned it. I didn't want you to find out this way."

"I think you didn't want me to find out at all. Or maybe you didn't even know."

"I just found out, but I want to discuss it with you."

Emily drew in a deep breath. She was so tired of all of it. Of battling herself to find a way back to him. Of trying to trust him again and feeling herself come up against a rock-solid, cold wall of resistance.

"I'm about to catch a plane to Nevada. There's not a lot to talk about, I think you can see all the reasons that this can't work. You should call an attorney soon and we can make this as smooth as possible for the girls," she said with finality.

"Nevada? Where are you—"

"I have to go."

She hung up and stood looking out the big glass window, at the planes waiting at the gates. The sky was a pale blue-gray, dark clouds were blowing in from the west.

She felt numb. It was as if all the sadness and anxiety she'd been struggling against, the endless circling questions in her mind about their marriage, their past and future, just evaporated like steam from a boiling kettle. She felt a slight sense of relief; she knew that would pass and the deep well of sorrow would pull her down again.

She knew better than anyone that grief was a process, it didn't go away, it just became a part of you. She had survived worse. She would survive the loss of her marriage. She would go on, like she always did. She didn't know how to do anything else.

. . .

Kaveri pulled into the parking garage of the luxury condominium complex in Brentwood, Sierra by her side in the passenger seat. The whole way there they'd been making small talk, aware that Mackenzie could hear what they were saying. Sierra had removed the tracker when they were a few blocks from home and left it in a park.

They rode the glistening elevator to the top floor and stepped out into a large, elegant penthouse.

"Wow! What is this place?" Kaveri asked, taking in the expensive furnishings.

"It's my escape plan. After my grandfather dies, I've decided to leave the compound. I want to live a life that's my own, not what my mom wants it to be."

"Can you do that?" Kaveri asked.

"Of course, so can you," Sierra replied, putting on a brave face, a confidence that she didn't quite own yet.

"Did you hear that gunshot yesterday?" Kaveri asked, her voice small with fear.

Sierra nodded. "Yes. I saw Rawley Jaynes leaving. He looked like hell."

"What do you think is going on?"

"I'm not sure but there are some people who I think can help us figure some things out," she said, holding up Emily Ray's business card.

"How did you get that?" Kaveri asked, impressed.

"It was when the senator arrived with his people. I knew she had to attend to them and she couldn't be watching me coming and going from her house. I know how to deactivate individual cameras in different rooms so I made sure she would never see me getting the card," Sierra said proudly.

"Do you think they can help us figure out what's going on?" Kaveri asked.

"I hope so. Let's call them and find out what they want."

THIRTY

The sun was beginning its descent to the west. In a few hours it would be dusk, the most dangerous time. Trina Eagan rolled her broken and battered body over onto one side.

The wind had carried away the top layers of sand and she had managed to move her arms and hands to push enough away that she could take shallow breaths of fresh air. She was alive, barely. The man who had left her here thought she was dead.

It was cold and she'd lain in that hole in the ground overnight and most of the day, though she had no idea what time it was. Everything hurt, she knew she had broken bones because some of her limbs didn't work correctly. On her side, she felt the searing pain of ribs that had to be busted, and her lungs felt like there was something inside them, like when she accidentally inhaled water at the local pool. She could hear her own breathing, a ragged whistle.

She rolled onto her stomach, unable to stand or sit upright. But she could crawl, drag herself toward the highway. She heard cars in the distance and followed it. She didn't know how long she'd been there. She didn't know where she was. She didn't remember anything beyond locking up the convenience store. She knew it was a man who had grabbed her and done this to her. She remembered his scent and the feel of his fleshy grip on her body.

Her mouth was dry, her tongue coated with dirt. Her eyelids were caked with it also, making it hard to see. She moved slowly towards a yucca tree, clawing at the ground with her broken fingers, pain shooting up her arms. She had to keep going, it would get dark, and the packs of coyotes would be out, looking for food. She'd grown up in the desert, surrounded by them. She'd seen them on her walk to school, from her front porch. She'd be damned if she died this way, as their holiday feast.

Then she heard voices. She raised her head and saw people, dressed in black, calling her name. Was this how death arrived, she wondered? She struggled to make noise, to call back. The black-clad figures came closer. She realized they were police officers. Now they were running toward her, shouting, waving. She heard her name. They touched her gingerly, gently moving her onto a stretcher, a tube stuck into her mouth. Water dripping onto her tongue. She thanked God, promising to get on better terms with him. She'd been saved.

Emily and Ryan buckled their seatbelts for the short flight to Las Vegas McCarran Airport. From there they would rent a car and drive to the Sanders' home, just across the Nevada border at Primm. Emily wanted to get in and out quickly. She'd reviewed all the information on the discovery of Danica Hansen and while some of it seemed to make sense to Ryan, she knew the truth. It was just an elaborate fabrication.

"When are we meeting with Elsbeth Winter to drop off the samples?" Ryan asked.

"Tomorrow. She's at UCLA at a conference so we don't have to go all the way to the Stemma Lab in Orange County."

"And we have to get the DNA from the Hansens down in South Bay," he added. "But I can do that."

"When?"

"Tomorrow morning. I'm single, I don't have anyone waiting for me at home. You have kids. Leave it to me."

Emily looked at him in gratitude. "Remember when I said you were a high-quality man? You really are."

"I'm glad you still feel that way after sleeping with me," he whispered, with a wicked grin.

"Shush! You are shameless!" She laughed. It felt good to laugh after her phone call with Antonio.

The pilot came over the PA system, advising them to put their seats in an upright position and to set their phone to Airplane mode. As Emily was about to set her phone a call came through. The number was unlisted, and she planned to let it go to voicemail, but she decided to answer it instead.

"May I speak to Special Agent Emily Ray?" The caller was young. And apprehensive.

"This is Emily Ray. Who's this?"

"This is Kaveri Miller Browne. I think you want to talk to me?"

Emily sat up, tapping Ryan's leg as she reached for a pen and paper in her bag.

"Yes, Ms. Browne. I've had some questions for you regarding your return home and how you came into contact with Rawley Jaynes."

Before Kaveri could answer, Sierra took the phone from her and said, "This is Sierra Miller Browne, Kaveri's mother. Could we set up a time to meet tomorrow?"

Stunned, Emily said, "Yes, tomorrow would be great. Where and when?"

"How is noon in Brentwood? I'll text you the address," Sierra said.

"Perfect. It will be me and my partner, Andrew Ryan."

"Okay. We'll see you then. We have some questions also," Sierra said cryptically, before hanging up.

An hour and a half later, Emily and Ryan pulled up outside the Sanders' home in Baker.

As they approached, Emily whispered, "You take the lead on

this, I just want to observe." She snapped the rubber band on her wrist several times and straightened her posture, like a soldier heading into battle.

The door was opened by Hilda Sanders, whose large frame blocked entry. She stared at them for a moment before asking, "Are you Jehovah's Witnesses?"

"No, ma'am. We're with the FBI. If it's okay, we just wanted to ask you a few questions about your daughter, Danica."

Hilda nodded. "Shirelle's out in the yard, I'll get her. We still call her Shirelle; all this other stuff has been very sudden for all of us. Come on in."

Emily and Ryan stepped into a simple but cozy living room. A spoon collection from different states hung in a special cabinet on one wall. A series of framed family photos from Sears or JCPenny were hung over the fireplace which was filled with empty cereal boxes. A La-Z-Boy recliner was covered with a George Strait decorative blanket. Hilda returned with Shirelle, the woman Rawley Jaynes appeared on television with as Danica Hansen.

"Hello, I'm Shirelle Sanders," she said, extending her hand.

She was shorter than Emily, probably five foot five at the most. She had a plain, chubby face and full lips. She was nervous, wiping her palms repeatedly on her jeans as she sat next to Hilda and looked to Emily and Ryan, her expression open but fearful.

"Thank you for talking to us, Danica, I know..." Ryan began, but Shirelle cut him off.

"Please call me Shirelle. I don't feel comfortable with the other name."

"Okay, Shirelle, we just wanted to know how you came into contact with Mr. Jaynes and how he told you about the possibility that you were Danica Hansen."

Shirelle drew in a deep breath and looked down at her hands. Emily saw that she was shaking.

"I've told this story now so many times..." Shirelle said, her voice breaking.

Emily felt a sudden wave of sympathy. She leaned forward and patted Shirelle's hand.

"It's okay. You don't have to tell us. We're investigating a possible fraud related to someone else that Jaynes worked with. You're not in any trouble, you haven't done anything wrong, okay?" Emily said, tenderly. Ryan looked at her in surprise.

"But maybe I have?" Shirelle asked, fighting tears.

"Shirelle, honey, why don't you go check on your dad in the bedroom?" Hilda suggested.

Once she was out of earshot, Hilda said, "There's just so much going on with all of this. That lady, Zanie, called Shirelle and told her not to talk to you FBI people but we got scared and thought we should."

"What can you tell us about how Shirelle came to live with you? We've read the information that Jaynes has put out about her past," Ryan said.

Hilda shook her head, folding her hands together on her stomach.

"My cousin, Coralee, was crazy. Just crazy and wild; had been her whole life. Always in trouble, always running with all kinds of boys. She was a fair bit younger than me. Roy and I were living in Kansas at the time. One day she calls up and says she's got this girl, wants to send her to visit us in the summer. I rarely talked to Coralee, you have to understand. We'd never heard of this child, suddenly she was coming to visit."

"Was Coralee her mother?" Emily asked.

"I thought so, how else would she get ahold of a child? But she claimed she wasn't the mother. She didn't want to be an adult, couldn't handle any responsibility. It makes me ill to think of the life that little kid had with her, especially with the epilepsy."

"Did she come to visit you in Kansas?" Ryan asked.

"No, that would've required money to send her. We decided to move out here when Roy got a new job with a different trucking company and we let Coralee know, just in case. Then about a year later, she just dropped her off with us and took off in an RV with some guy who worked in those traveling amusement parks. No birth certificate, when we looked for one, we found out she'd never registered the birth. It was like Shirelle didn't exist."

"So, you took her in and started calling her Shirelle Sanders?" Emily asked.

"Yes. And when she needed to get a social security number, we... lied about that. We did an affidavit saying that we were there when she was born and we got a midwife we know to go along. Is that why you're here?" Hilda asked, fearfully.

"No, there'll be no trouble with that at all. Don't worry. We're retesting the DNA on the people that Rawley Jaynes found, to be sure that it's valid," Emily explained.

Shirelle came back in; it was clear she had been listening from the hallway.

"You think it could be false?" she asked.

"We don't know. We have to talk to the Hansen family as well, but we want to be sure. If you're willing, of course," Ryan said.

"Sure, I'll do it. But what about the money?" Shirelle asked.

"What money?" Emily asked, with a glance to Ryan.

"The victim's fund money. Mr. Jaynes said it was for victims of kidnappings when they're found, from the state. We're using it for my dad's cancer treatment," Shirelle explained.

"I don't think there will be any problem with that," Emily said. Ryan shot her a wary look.

"But if the DNA isn't a real match, we have to give the money back. It wouldn't be right to keep it," Hilda said.

Emily excused herself to use the bathroom. She needed to get out of the room with Shirelle and Hilda. She had arrived with her guard up, prepared to deal with people who were part of an elaborate con game and instead, she found an awkward, frightened woman who was clearly traumatized by a childhood with an unstable parent. Just like she had been with her real mother, Amber Hansen.

It was obvious that the Sanders family had been tricked and manipulated by Jaynes. The idea that they would return the money they were using for Roy's medical treatment was more than Emily could bear. In the bathroom she splashed cold water on her face, pressing the palms of her hands against her eyes, as if she could push the tears back in.

When she returned to the living room, Ryan was collecting Shirelle's DNA sample and placing it in the sealed bag.

"I don't want you to worry about the money or anything. We're just doing this to follow up with a different case. It has nothing to do with you. It's about Mr. Jaynes," Emily reassured them.

As they left, Shirelle followed them outside.

"I don't like to upset my mom; this whole thing has been so strange. But I don't think of myself as Danica Hansen. I don't know who that is. I know I could be her, and I figure if Mr. Jaynes found me, he must have some reasons to believe that I'm her," she said, looking over her shoulder. "I don't like those two Hansen ladies. I met them once and I... just don't like them."

"Well, there's not much to like about them," Emily said before she could stop herself.

"I just want everything to be the way it was, living here with my mom and dad. But now I'm worried about the money. There's no other way to pay for my dad's treatment. He's got that Non-Hodgkin lymphoma."

Emily stepped close to her and took her hand. "Nothing has to change for you, even if the DNA comes back as a match, okay? You don't have to go on television shows with Mr. Jaynes or see the Hansen family. You have a right to your privacy, okay?"

"I'm worried about my dad," she said, on the verge of tears again.

"Don't worry about it. I promise it will all be fine," Emily said.

She and Ryan got into the car and drove away. For Shirelle Sanders, being Danica Hansen was no longer a liability. It was a miracle that could save her father's life.

THIRTY-ONE

After flying back to Ontario, Emily and Ryan were driving toward Los Angeles, through the small cities of the Inland Empire, when his phone rang. He set it to speaker mode.

"Agent Ryan? This is officer Cortez from Salton City. We found Trina Eagan."

"Is she alive?"

"Yes, barely. Whoever attacked her thought she was dead and buried her in a shallow grave, way out in the desert. We think it was Rawley Jaynes."

Ryan gripped the steering wheel in fury, Emily touched his arm gently.

"Could she identify who hurt her?" Emily asked.

"No, someone grabbed her from behind but we're processing Jaynes' car. I'm sure we'll find some of her DNA," Cortez said. Ryan thanked him and hung up. He turned to Emily.

"At least Trina is alive. What time do you want to meet up to drop the DNA with Elsbeth?" he asked.

"I'll check with her, and we can meet her at UCLA. I hope she can run a rapid test right away."

She felt Shirelle Sanders' DNA kit burning a hole in her purse.

. . .

Gerte carried the tray of beef consommé into Jinx's room. Sozi was ready for her dinner break and Gerte was to handle his evening meal. After the girl left, she sat next to the old man's bed and moved his tray into position. She helped him sit up properly and tucked a napkin into his pajama top.

"Are you ready for a nice dinner, Mr. Jinx?" she said pleasantly.

He remained impassive, staring at the television blankly.

"Do you have an appetite today?" she asked, spooning the hot broth into his mouth. He pulled back; it was too hot. It burned him but she held his head in place.

"*Willst du eine gute Zeit Haben?*" she asked, intimately.

His eyes flickered to her, a shadow of recognition. She forced another spoon of soup into his mouth.

"Too hot? That's too bad. When I saw your friend the other day, the senator, I remembered things I had forgotten for a long time. I wonder, do you remember them?"

She leaned in close to his face and repeated, "*Willst du eine gute Zeit haben?*"

She prepared another spoon of the steaming soup.

"You know, I wanted to come up here and just end it for you. But that would be too kind, after what you did to me, to Ilse and Lucille. Johan. And how much you hurt your own children? How many things did I see in all these years?"

She could tell that he understood her; he blinked rapidly at her and she saw fear in his eyes. She waved the spoon in front of him, the steam rising.

"No, this will not be quick and easy, Mr. Jinx. You know, because I'm fat and stupid. Like a farm animal, remember? Eat up, we have a whole bowl to finish..."

After dropping Ryan at his car at the Burbank Studios, Emily headed home, exhausted and emotionally empty. The day had been relentless and so many things had happened in the last twenty-four hours, her brain was on system overload. She pulled into the driveway watching the big gates close behind her. As she stepped into the foyer, she imagined Anjelica standing in the same spot, wondering if she realized how hard won this life was for them? Moose trotted up to her and she patted his big head, absentmindedly.

Antonio was in the kitchen, waiting for her as she'd expected and dreaded.

"How was Nevada?" he asked, taking a sip from a bottle of Corona.

"Fine. I'm tired, it's been an impossible day," she replied, dropping her bag and moving to the gun safe to lock up her Glock, and to avoid meeting his eyes.

"Are you hungry?" He gestured to one of the kitchen bar stools for her to sit down. She remained standing.

"No, I ate already."

They stood in awkward silence for a few beats then she turned to head upstairs. He reached out, taking her arm.

"Emily, I want to talk about this..."

She turned on him, overcoming her exhaustion, in full fight or flight mode.

"About what? You lied when you told me you didn't have intercourse with her. You've lied again and again, and you only confess when you've been exposed! I can't do this."

"I'm not even sure this baby is mine," he said.

"But it could be, right? Which means you didn't even use protection. You just raw dogged it with a woman you haven't seen in years and planned to come home to me? It can't be fixed. Stop trying!" She gripped the banister to keep herself standing.

He hung his head; his hands were shaking as he covered his eyes.

"I have to be able to fix this, we have to fix this..." he stammered.

"No, we don't. And you know what I think? You wanted this to happen. You did something that you knew would break us. But you didn't want to have to make that decision, so you forced me to."

"That's not true, Emily. I don't want this!"

"You loved all of this as long as I was Emily Ray, the amazing girl who overcame so much. But once I told you who I really was, how I'd hidden that secret for so long, this is what you did. Once I was Danica Hansen, I didn't matter that much anymore. None of this mattered anymore!"

She burst into tears of frustration and pain, unable to hold them back. She had said it, out loud, for everyone to hear. The wound that would never heal, no matter how many castles she built on top of it. She wiped her eyes on the sleeve of her jacket.

"Please, just let this go. Let me go. I can't do this anymore..." she whispered.

He nodded, stepping back away from her.

"Okay. I'm sorry, Emily. I really am."

She turned without a word and climbed the stairway. He watched her, realizing for the first time, that she was far beyond his reach.

Emily walked into the bathroom and stood at the sink in her slippers. She'd stripped down for a shower and now wore just her chenille robe. She thought back to Shirelle Sanders' tormented eyes, pleading with them.

There's no other way to pay for my dad's treatment...

She reached into her bag and pulled the DNA kit out with Danica's sample and stuck it in a drawer. She picked up a new kit and took the fresh swab out. She looked at herself in the mirror, her mascara forming dark circles under her eyes where her tears had made it run.

Then she put the swab in her mouth and ran it in a circular motion before putting it in the plastic bag and marking it, *Danica Hansen*. She put the bag back into her purse to drop off with Elsbeth Winter the next day.

THIRTY-TWO

Rawley Jaynes sat in the back of a police car, sweating despite the frigid air conditioning. He was being transferred to the jail in Riverside County. No one told him why or how it had happened but he didn't care. So far, he hadn't said anything, even though he knew they would find DNA for both Brittney and Trina in his trunk. He prayed they wouldn't find the bodies. Brittney would be harder to locate, but he had been in a rush with Trina. He'd only dug a little over a foot down into the sand and covered her. If scavengers found her and dragged her body parts too soon, the cops would be able to identify her.

He wished he'd been able to call Zanie when they arrested him; she would've known what to do. But she was dead in the big freezer back at his house in Calabasas. He knew they were pulling search warrants and feared it was just a matter of time until they found her body. He felt the strong urge to urinate; it was a stress response when his bladder would get reactive and his heartburn would rage, making him squirm with discomfort.

He had called a few lawyer friends who had helped him out in the past but none had called back. He also called Mackenzie, letting her know about his arrest. He was sure she would intervene to protect her reputation and send over a high-priced Beverly Hills attorney to handle his case and get him off. He wasn't worried. He always landed on his feet.

At nine a.m. Ryan pulled up at the Applebee's Restaurant in Torrance, where he'd agreed to meet Amber Hansen and her sister, Janelle. He walked in and scanned the room. He recognized them from photos he'd pulled up online. They were seated at the bar, even at this early hour. Both women were faded blondes who'd spent too much time in the sun. They waved at him as he approached.

"Are you Agent Ryan?" Amber asked. "You're a lot younger than I thought!"

"What're you drinking?" Janelle asked.

"Nothing. It's nine a.m. I'm here to get DNA from you, Mrs. Hansen."

Janelle laughed loudly; he could tell she was already tipsy.

"He says that like you're his third-grade teacher! Mrs. Hansen!"

"Why're we doing this, anyway? We did it already for Rawley," Amber complained.

"Because we are running the DNA again," he replied, handing her a swab.

She and Janelle suddenly looked nervous as she ran the swab around her mouth.

"Why again? Is there a problem?" Amber asked.

"I don't know. You tell me, is there?" he said, looking directly at her and taking the swab from her hand.

"Whatever. This is the last time I'm doing it. And tell Rawley to call me, I need to speak to him," Amber said, sullenly.

"That will be difficult. He's been detained in a fraud investigation. I don't think he's calling you," Ryan said, turning to go.

. . .

The next day, Mackenzie opened the curtains in her bedroom, overlooking the rose garden. It was a beautiful sunny December day, the kind that people in the Midwest and East can only dream about. She'd slept well, especially after waking with an alarm at three a.m. to leave a message for Gideon, in Tel Aviv. It was simple and to the point.

Open the gates

And that was it. She knew that within a few hours Harry Hubbard's career would be over, and he'd be out of their lives forever. She'd seen the information that Gideon had on Hubbard, and it was at a level of illegality there was no way he could spin the way he usually did: deflect, deny, dismiss.

Hubbard would be exposed for what he was and had always been. There would be a resignation and most likely, an arrest. A trial covered by every news outlet around the world. His party, running wild with neo-fascism, would sacrifice him to the political hyenas; he would be the fresh meat they dined on for months. A pariah, rejected by everyone, on both sides of the aisle.

Sierra had let her know that she and Kaveri would be out shopping today at the Brentwood Country Mart. Mackenzie was pleased that they were spending more time together, maybe Sierra would come around to everything sooner than expected. Mackenzie would plan a celebratory dinner and ask Chef Michel to prepare a range of special dishes.

She'd pulled some strings to have Rawley moved to Riverside, where it would be much easier to get things dealt with. And Melanie Lichtman had landed in Nicaragua, thinking she had gone off the radar by traveling a two-and-a-half-hour drive from Playas Maderas, on the Carretera Panamericana. She was staying in a rented cabana on the beach. Casa de Las Piedras.

It was a good day.

. . .

In his townhouse in Washington, Harry Hubbard was deciding which tie to wear with his robin's egg blue dress shirt. The lavender was nice, but the black was more dramatic. His phone on the dresser began buzzing. He ignored it, it was probably the office of constituent services wanting to arrange a tour or some other dry-as-dust event. He chose the black tie and began tying it around his shirt collar. The phone kept buzzing. Exasperated, he answered it.

"This better be worth it!" he barked.

On the other end of the line, his office chief of staff was trying to speak to him, but he kept losing the words.

"Senator, you have to... turn it... turn on... on the news right now! There's a... story in... about you. Several stories... really... I don't know what to do..."

Hubbard flipped the TV on and saw his image, in boxer shorts, holding a drink with his arm thrown over the shoulders of a young teenage boy. The video included other guests and teens with their faces blacked out, in various states of intoxication. Hubbard froze, dropping his black tie to the floor. Uriel had agreed to keep these images secret if his price was met. Hubbard still had several weeks left and Jinx was about to die.

But someone had done an end run around him, discovering the collateral his adversary held in emotional escrow. He remembered the way Mackenzie Miller Browne had pulled her hand away from his at the compound. How she had produced Kaveri at the critical moment. He'd underestimated her.

Emily arrived at the FBI offices early to organize the information they had compiled in the investigation, in preparation to present to SAC Powers in the next twenty-four hours. Ryan was already there with the DNA sample from Amber Hansen.

"How'd it go?" Emily asked.

"Fine. They were seated at the bar in Applebee's, at nine in the morning," he said dryly.

She felt lighter today than she had in weeks. She knew it

wouldn't last but it was the freedom from uncertainty with Antonio. She'd let go of the struggle and made a choice. She had a direction to move forward toward which felt better than stagnating in sorrow. They would meet Elsbeth Winter at eleven to drop off Danica's DNA sample and then go to see Kaveri and Sierra Browne.

Stephanie Leedom burst into their office. "Did you see the news about Senator Hubbard! It's insane!"

Emily and Ryan turned on the television to see a live broadcast revealing the indiscretions and illegal behavior of Senator Harry Hubbard. The newscaster continued her report as more inappropriate images filled the screen, the faces of minors obscured.

"The longtime southern senator has been the focus of rumors regarding his personal life. Unmarried, he has been a stalwart pillar of the Republican Party for decades. But with this new scandal, there are few in Washington who believe he can recover. Facing arrest and charges for a range of crimes against children, many say that the long career of Harry Hubbard is now over..."

Emily watched in shock as Hubbard's behavior was exposed. She knew that these allegations were tied somehow to his inquiry about Kaveri. Emily figured SAC Powers had been caught in the crossfire and if it leaked that he'd been doing a political favor to a disgraced pedophile, his career would be over as well.

She didn't feel any sympathy for him, not after he refused to do the right thing when Trina Eagan went missing. He was a political animal, like all the rest, using his power in all the wrong ways. She only hoped his behavior hadn't damaged Ryan's faith in his work. She didn't want to see him hurt or disillusioned, which she found oddly comforting. It meant that even with Antonio's deception, she still had a tender heart, underneath her defenses, and she had worked hard to find and nurture it. She was not as broken as she thought.

. . .

The news had been playing all morning in the big house. Gerte saw that the senator and good friend of Jinx Doucette-Browne was being destroyed as his crimes were revealed to the world. She knew that they predated anything they were showing on the news, he had been getting away with them for over fifty years. But today was the judgment day, the day of retribution, when the wicked shall be cast down.

She carried the Malt-O-Meal hot cereal and asked Sozi to help bring up the laundry while she took care of Mr. Jinx's breakfast. He was still on his back in bed as she set up his tray and utensils, pouring the warm milk and cinnamon into his porridge. She poured weak tea from the silver pot, with just a dash of crème. A small plate of applesauce with a squeeze of lemon, all the things Mr. Jinx preferred. Then she turned to him and leaned over his prone body, her face close to his.

She took one of the bed pillows and whispered, "*Willst du eine gute Zeit Haben?*"

She pressed the pillow against his face, smothering the life out of him. He was so weak, his flailing body felt like a baby bird, struggling in her palm. She held the pillow until he was quiet and still.

Then she said, "I forgot your napkin, Mr. Jinx. You've drooled a bit. I'll be right back."

Emily and Ryan stood outside Teresaki Science building on the UCLA campus. It was crowded as usual with a student body of forty-eight thousand. Emily had attended college there and felt a sense of nostalgia, remembering her days racing across the huge campus on a bike. Elsbeth emerged and waved, beaming a big smile at Emily.

"Emily! So good to see you!" She hugged her and turned to Ryan.

"Elsbeth, this is my partner, Special Agent Andrew Ryan."

They exchanged a handshake, and she asked, "So, what're we doing?"

Emily explained the situation with Rawley Jaynes, the unofficial inquiry they were undertaking and their need to see if Danica Hansen was legitimate.

"I'm working in a lab here today, showing students how we do rapid DNA for criminal procedures and such. I'll run these right away, I'll have answers in a few hours."

Emily and Ryan left, walking among the students, feeling distinctly out of place with so many young kids.

"How'd things go at home last night?" Ryan asked.

"Hard. But I've had enough and I told him, it's done. It's over."

"I'm sorry."

"Don't be. You didn't do anything, except make it easier," she said.

Ryan smiled and reached down, linking his fingers with hers as they strolled across campus.

An hour later they were waiting outside Sierra's condo in Brentwood. The news about Harry Hubbard continued to grow, with new allegations made by a young male sex worker in Washington D.C. who claimed Hubbard was a fixture in the pick-up bars. Emily predicted he would be resigning within the day.

When they saw Kaveri's BMW pull into the underground parking lot, they went to the main entrance and entered the code that Sierra had given them. They rode the elevator to the top floor and stepped out into a spacious hallway. They found Sierra's unit number and knocked on the door. Sierra Miller Browne opened the door, bearing a strong resemblance to her mother, albeit with a more bohemian style, her blond hair flowing freely down her back.

"Come in, I'm Sierra. This is Kaveri," she said.

The tall, pretty young woman nodded in greeting. Sierra guided them to the living room that had stunning 360-degree views to downtown and the beach.

"Kaveri and I have some questions, and I think you have some as well. You came to the compound and spoke to my mother, Mackenzie?" Sierra asked.

"We were doing an unofficial inquiry requested of our office, regarding the legitimacy of your daughter, Kaveri, given her long absence and abduction."

"Who asked for it?"

"Senator Harry Hubbard, who seemed to have some ties to your grandfather."

Kaveri fidgeted and crossed her legs. "But why would someone think I'm not really me? Mr. Jaynes took the DNA and everything and Mackenzie said it was a match."

"We're retesting the DNA on Danica Hansen due to some doubts about Mr. Jaynes' methods. But the thing we're looking for is motive as to why the DNA might have been faked."

"I think it has to do with my mother and the estate. That's all she cares about. The details are in the trust. I've been trying to get ahold of the documents, but my mother has blocked me," Sierra said.

"Do you know of any way that we could get access to the trust documents?" Ryan asked.

"My mother is watching me like a hawk these days, but you could try Ben Wershow. He was one of the financial advisory team and he stopped working with our accounts last year. He's a nice man, very honest, and I think he became seriously ill. I have his home number if you want to call him," Sierra said, writing the number down and handing it to Emily.

"So, do I have to do the DNA test again? What if it's not a match this time?" Kaveri asked; her anxiety was obvious.

Emily shook her head. "You don't have to consent to anything, Kaveri. This isn't a formal investigation. No one is bringing charges of any kind against anyone. This is simply a personal favor that was requested of our office."

Kaveri looked skeptical and turned to Sierra for guidance. In Sierra's eyes, Emily saw the moment that she made the decision.

"We're not going to be doing that. Kaveri is home now, where she belongs. We have a lot of plans to put together for the future," Sierra said, sliding an arm around Kaveri's shoulders.

THIRTY-THREE

As they rode the elevator down, Ryan said, "Everything in this case keeps knocking me down. I expect to feel one way, then I meet the people, and I feel completely different. I feel sorry for Kaveri and Sierra, like they're fighting against this evil empire!"

"I agree. Life is like that, way more complex that we first think it is."

In the car, Emily dialed the number for Ben Wershow. After a few rings, a scratchy, weak voice answered.

"I'm trying to reach Ben Wershow," Emily said.

"What do you want? I'm very sick and I don't have much energy."

"I'm Special Agent Emily Ray with the FBI. My partner and I need to find out some information about the Doucette-Browne estate. Sierra Miller Browne gave us your number."

Ben laughed weakly, erupting in a fit of coughing.

"She's the only normal one in the family. I'd love to spill the tea on those assholes. I'm home, I can't go anywhere. Come on by."

Half an hour later, Emily and Ryan sat across from Ben Wershow in his Century City condominium. He wore thick pajamas and a knit cap on his head.

"I'm not well, so let's not beat around the bush, okay? What do you want to know about the Doucette-Brownes?"

"You might have heard that Kaveri Browne was found recently?" Emily asked.

Wershow nodded. "Oh yeah. Well, Mackenzie had to produce her. If not, the money wouldn't stay in the family. It'll go to that loathsome senator, the one who's going down in flames today. Thick as thieves those two old dirtbags." He was seized with coughing and put a napkin to his lips.

"What do you mean?" Ryan asked.

Wershow shrugged. "The old man has it in the will that there must be an heir, in the fourth generation. Mackenzie is his only daughter left and when Connor died, Sierra was the only grandkid. When Kaveri went missing, they probably thought she'd have more kids, but she didn't. So, earlier this year, when the old man's health took a nosedive, Mackenzie needed to find Kaveri, otherwise Hubbard would get his hands on a huge portion of the estate."

Emily nodded. It was like Ken Carlisle said, Jaynes found Kaveri because he had to. She was certain Kaveri was not who they claimed she was. She was Megan Hoard, from a shithole blip on the map, in the middle of the desert, with a mother probably very similar to Amber Hansen. But Kaveri Browne never needed to know that truth.

Wershow was seized with another coughing fit that left him pale and barely upright in his chair.

"Could you guys give me Sierra's number? She was always a nice kid, and I don't have much time left. I'd love to say goodbye to her," Wershow said.

Gerte stood with a weeping Sozi and the other staff as Jinx Doucette-Browne's body was wheeled out of the big house. Mackenzie watched from the stairway, her arms crossed, her face impassive. Sozi had been the one to find him. She thought he was asleep at first but then she realized his monitors were flatlining.

The alarms had not gone off. She screamed and the rest of the staff came running.

When the mortuary staff picked up his body to put into the bag for transport, he was like a piece of tissue paper, chalk white and almost transparent. Gerte stared as the bag zipped closed over his face, swallowing him up in darkness, where he belonged. When they wheeled the body out, Mackenzie came down and shut the door behind him.

She turned to the staff and said, "You can all take the rest of the day off, due to the shock you have all suffered. Tomorrow, I want the house hung with black crepe and the mirrors covered. We will observe one month of mourning for my father. As soon as the lawyers have the memorial service planned, I will inform all of you. Thank you."

She retreated to her bedroom and shut the door. The house was quiet, deathly quiet. She lay down on her big bed and closed her eyes. It was over, finally she was free.

A smile crept over her face as she drifted peacefully to sleep, as if for the first time in her life.

"I've got the DNA back," Elsbeth said, seated across from Emily and Ryan at Boondock's Coffee Roasters in Westwood. Elsbeth held several sheets of paper with lines and markers in long columns.

"What does Danica's DNA show?" Ryan asked.

"She's a match. She's the daughter of Amber Hansen."

Emily feigned surprise while Ryan broke into a huge smile. She knew it would match, and the Sanders would keep the money for Roy's treatment. She'd made sure of it, and she had no regrets.

"So, now we compile our report for Powers and confirm that Kaveri Miller Browne is legitimate. And this is over," Ryan said.

"This whole thing sounds like a movie or something!" Elsbeth said. "You always have such exciting cases, Emily."

Emily smiled. "I say I want a quiet, calm life but these things keep dropping into my lap."

Ryan looked at her in surprise. "You, quiet and calm? You're the GOAT, Emily. You'd be bored stiff with quiet and calm."

Emily nodded, he was right. She realized he understood her better than she thought he did.

Harry Hubbard hadn't left his house that morning, in his robin's egg blue dress shirt. He'd been pacing calling his attorney who wasn't calling him back. He'd texted his colleagues and long-time friends in the Senate but there was no response. Already a number of organizations he'd been affiliated with had publicly broken ties with him. He heard he was going to be stripped of leadership roles in several important committees. And the accusations kept coming.

By late afternoon, there were seven young men who had come forward to detail his interactions with them, from the poppers and cocaine to the romps at the Hotel Pearl that had once been his playground. Parents of two minors were filing charges, the police were investigating, maybe the FBI would join them. Hubbard paced his house, cursing whoever had given incriminating images to Uriel and his handlers. Cursing Mackenzie for discovering the clause in the will, for conveniently producing a long-lost heir at the eleventh hour. And cursing Jinx Doucette-Browne for clinging to life beyond a reasonable age and not dying and making everyone's life easier. He hated them all. He hated himself.

He reached onto the high shelf in his closet and pulled down a 9-millimeter Glock. He walked into his gray marble bathroom and smoothed his hair into place. He still wore his dress shirt from the morning. He began to hum the Aggie War Hymn from his university days. He smiled his best campaign smile, flashing his dazzling veneers. Then he pulled the trigger.

. . .

Sierra dropped Kaveri off and went back to her own house on the quadrangle. She'd spoken to Ben Wershow and she'd texted her mother to arrange a meeting. She found Mackenzie seated in the sunroom.

"What is this about, Sierra?" Mackenzie asked.

"I know what you wanted from Kaveri. How you needed a fourth-generation heir to keep the estate in our hands. A large part of it would've gone to Harry Hubbard otherwise," she said.

"Yes, and it would've been used to cover up his criminal activities that are now exposed."

"Mom, I don't remember a lot about the day Kaveri went missing but I know you do. I need to know what happened. I need you to tell me the truth."

Mackenzie looked long and hard at her daughter. Everyone was gone, Sierra was all she had left. Mackenzie sat slowly on a chair at the window, overlooking the Japanese garden.

"She drowned, you and I were with her, at the pool," she said simply. "I had to take a call on the landline in the house, and I left her with you. You were so high you didn't know what was going on. She fell in... and drowned," Mackenzie's voice trembled at the memory. Her gaze was heavy with sorrow as she stared out the window. "I pulled her out, but she was gone. I know you won't believe it, but Kaveri was a new beginning for us, the whole family. With Connor gone, she was the hope that remained."

Sierra stood still, frozen with shock and crushing remorse that she had played a part in her daughter's death, that her drug use had rendered her so unaware that she hadn't noticed when Kaveri drowned. Just the thought of how it must have unfolded made her feel dizzy and sick. She stumbled as she sat on the couch, unable to keep her balance under the weight of the truth. She struggled to speak.

"What happened... after that?"

Mackenzie scoffed bitterly. "Your grandfather was afraid we'd be charged and he said we had to hide it. He said one more tragic death would ruin the reputation of the family. So, we could not mourn her, we could not acknowledge her. He made everyone agree to say that she was abducted. He was a different man in those days, no one dared to challenge him. So, we buried her in an unmarked grave out in the bone orchard. You used to walk out there at night, in circles for hours."

Sierra had hazy memories of keeping that vigil when she returned from an extended rehab stay in Brazil, after Kaveri's death. The treatment center had tried all manner of medications and interventions on her and by the time she returned home, her brain was scrambled. But she could recall walking in endless circles in the bone orchard, in the dead of night, following the path of her own, private labyrinth.

Mackenzie turned a pleading gaze to her. "And then when I learned about the clause in the will, I knew I had to do something to protect the inheritance. And that meant bringing Kaveri back to life."

"With the help of Rawley Jaynes?"

"Yes. He's good at these types of things. He saved your brother from being charged in that drug case, he stole the evidence. He covered for him in the murder of that drug dealer. He found a good candidate to replace Kaveri. It cost me a lot of money but as you take over this estate, you'll see it's good to have someone like Jaynes in your pocket. You must have a lot of helpers, to neutralize threats," Mackenzie said with an easy smile. "Rawley Jaynes will never darken our door again. Someone is taking care of him today in the Riverside County jail, it will look like a fatal fight among inmates."

Sierra stared at her mother, stunned at how easily she discarded people she deemed a threat to her power and comfort. Who had value in her twisted universe and who did not.

"So, you were ready to have this young girl just become Kaveri, to meet your ends?"

"Yes, I was. And now, we don't need her anymore, you see? She protected the estate and now your grandfather and Hubbard are dead. I kept it all in the family. We can send her on her way with a cash gift. We can say that she's studying abroad."

"Kaveri's real name is Megan Hoard, isn't it? How much did her mother take to deny her? To say she wasn't really her child, to fit your plan?"

Mackenzie laughed softly. "It was a bargain. Just thirty thousand dollars. I had to pay the others more. Can you imagine? A small investment to save billions."

She looked to Sierra, her eyes shining with satisfaction.

"Do you really think this is all over now?" Sierra asked, incredulously.

"This is a new beginning for us. A new era for the family. I did everything right. I've steered this family through every storm. We'll get through this together, Sierra."

Sierra nodded and moved to her mother, gently taking her hands and looking into her eyes.

"Mom, I need you to understand how this is going to work."

Mackenzie smiled softly at her, grasping her daughter's hands tightly, "I knew you'd understand, Sierra. We can make all of this right, together."

"We're not getting rid of Kaveri. You made her into my daughter and that is who she is now. You are never telling her the truth of what you did. You are never sending her back to a family that sold her for less than the cost of a new car," Sierra said, her voice breaking at the sadness of it.

"But she's just a nothing, a girl from nowhere!" Mackenzie protested.

"She's the heir to the Doucette-Browne estate," Sierra said with growing confidence. "And you are moving abroad, within the month. I don't care where you go. You'll live in luxury, but you'll stay gone. I'll make proper funeral arrangements when you die. If you ever try to come back or hurt us in any way, I will tell the police everything you did over the years with Rawley Jaynes, and you'll go to prison."

Mackenzie blanched and began to object, but something in Sierra's eyes told her it was over.

The meeting with SAC Powers was brief and blunt. He sat at his desk, across from Emily and Ryan, his face pale and drawn, his words clipped.

"There is no need for you to continue with the inquiry now that Senator Hubbard is dead. The privacy of the grieving Doucette-Browne family is to be respected and no further contact with them is to be made."

"What about the related illegalities in the Public Records office in Sacramento? The near-lethal assault on Trina Eagan? The suspicious death of Louise Niedermeier?" Emily asked.

Powers shifted uncomfortably in his big leather desk chair.

"We can refer those issues to local law enforcement. I'm sure they will appropriately deal with any crimes that have been committed. You can both return to your respective divisions now."

Emily and Ryan stood as Powers awkwardly shook their hands.

"Thank you both for your work on this," he said.

"You're welcome, sir, and may I express my condolences at the loss of your longtime friend, Senator Hubbard," Ryan said, with just enough edge in his voice to make Powers flinch.

An hour later, Emily and Ryan were heading home early, riding the elevator down to the first floor of the federal building.

"You did very good work on this. Thank you," Emily said.

"I just followed your lead. But I wanted to know, what did you mean yesterday, when you said that maybe Danica Hansen didn't want to be found?"

Emily considered for a moment, then replied carefully. "I meant that maybe there's a girl out there... somewhere, who was taken and never found. She's a woman now, who's living a different life than the one she was supposed to live. Maybe she worked hard to build it... and it's a better life."

He looked at her for a long beat, then said, "I think I understand."

They stepped out into the afternoon sunlight, splashing across the plaza.

"If I don't see you before Christmas, have a good holiday," Emily said.

"You, too. Next year will be better than this one," Ryan said.

They stood together but apart, in silence but with so many words barely balancing on their lips, waiting to be spoken.

"Well, I'm off. Drive safely," Emily said, turning and walking away toward the parking lot. Ryan watched her go for a long moment, then turned toward his car as the sun slipped slightly lower in the sky.

EPILOGUE

Seven fire engines stood on the grounds of the Doucette-Browne estate, but they were not enough to stop the flames. Somehow, several fires had erupted together, in the big house and the homes in the quadrangle. The fire chief expected an electrical explosion of some kind, but an extensive investigation would be required. For now, the property that had loomed so large in so many lives was burning down to ashes.

Sierra stood with Kaveri, watching the dark smoke billow up into the dusky sky, her eyes alight with a strange kind of wonder. She felt a sense of peace she had been searching for her entire life. With Kaveri at her side, she saw a path to redemption. A way to heal the damage that her family had caused to themselves and to others. A chance to be the breaker of generational curses, to change the course of the family legacy. Like her name, Kaveri was a river that would carry them to a new and different shore.

Mackenzie sat in horror, watching the fire, with her maid Luisa wrapping a blanket around her. The sirens of more engines filled the neighborhood as they approached, and news crews filmed from beyond the gates.

Under the shade of a willow tree, standing in shadow, Gerte

Brose smiled. They were all being set free in the magnificent blaze that would light the night sky for hours, like a clarion call announcing a new day.

A LETTER FROM THE AUTHOR

Dear Readers,

Thank you so much for reading *The Girl from Nowhere*! If you want to stay in touch with other readers and keep up to date on my new releases, please sign up for my email newsletter which will have the latest information on the Emily Ray series and more.

www.stormpublishing.co/michele-dominguez-greene

If you enjoyed the book and could spare a few moments to leave a review I would greatly appreciate it. Even a short review can help build an audience for a new book and ensure that it reaches as many readers as possible. Your support as readers is the lifeblood of any new book. Thank you so much!

I'll be posting updates and information to all my social media accounts and on my website, where readers can leave a message or comment, which I always look forward to reading, and I try to respond to all if time permits. Thank you!

Michele-Greene.com

instagram.com/micheledgreene

facebook.com/MGreeneArtist

x.com/MicheleDGreene

ACKNOWLEDGMENTS

My deepest gratitude to the amazing team at Storm Publishing, especially my editor, Claire Bord, for supporting this book series and expanding the story of Emily Ray in her journey of recovery. I would like to thank the brave women who shared their stories of childhood trauma with me to help me bring Emily's CPTSD to life. My agent, Jill Marsal, was a tremendous support through the challenging schedule I had this year with multiple books and deadlines. And my wonderful son, José Daniel, who makes every single day a million times better just by existing, the brightest star in my universe, forever.